As soon as he was gone, I leaned [over?] Eloise and whispered, "Don't invit[e] [diffe]rent my room. Don't you k[now] [everything's running] loose around here[?] [we] know."

She just laughed. "[sugar]. I was trying to improve your life[.] [H]e could be just right for you."

For a moment I was actually speechless. Aside from the fact that she's had four husbands of her own, not one of the couples she's thrown together has lived happily ever after.

"For God's sake, Eloise! He was wearing an earring. He's probably a professional knee buster."

"That last man of yours looked like Beaver Cleaver's big brother, too. You can't tell by the clothes they wear, sugar. It takes experience, and I've got it. Maybe this Wayne Holland is just the one you've been looking for."

"And maybe I've got a live chicken in my pocket." I said, shoving another filter full of Maxwell House in the coffee maker.

Also by Deborah Adams
Published by Ballantine Books:

ALL THE GREAT PRETENDERS
ALL THE CRAZY WINTERS

ALL THE DARK DISGUISES

Deborah Adams

BALLANTINE BOOKS • NEW YORK

Copyright © 1993 by Deborah Adams

All rights reserved under International and Pan-American Copyright Conventions. Published in the United States of America by Ballantine Books, a division of Random House, Inc., New York, and simultaneously in Canada by Random House of Canada Limited, Toronto.

Library of Congress Catalog Card Number: 92-97050

ISBN 0-345-37765-6

Manufactured in the United States of America

First Edition: March 1993

A DEDICATION POEM FOR SHARYN AND JOE

Roses are red,
Violets are blue.
Good bras are supportive,
and so are y'all.

Author's Note

In this book I have suggested that the town of Jesus Creek and the community of Plant are neighbors. In fact, Plant exists peacefully among the hills of Middle Tennessee, while Jesus Creek is located some twelve million light-years farther south.

Several people contributed to the research for this book by sharing their knowledge and experience. I offer my sincere thanks to Jack Blue, Officer Ken Combs, Lydia Corbitt, David Hunter, Pamela Hughes, and Kelly Willhite.

CHAPTER

1

The Fool: The journey has begun—now you must choose between right and wrong.

IN JESUS CREEK WE BELIEVE IN LEPRE-chauns. It's not necessarily a requirement for citizenship, but some people would have it so. Naturally we celebrate St. Patrick's Day with a vengeance, so things start popping in early February and no one settles down until after the big parade and attendant festivities. Phony brogues, green beer, grown men wearing top hats adorned with shamrocks—if I didn't enjoy parades and picnics so much myself, I'd find it ridiculous.

As you might have guessed, most employees in our area of Angela County are excused from work, with pay, in order to participate in events related to the holiday. I don't get the day off, paid or otherwise, because I'm the newest staff member at Eloise's Diner, and Eloise never closes. ("But, Kay, if you've got a date for the parade . . ." Eloise had said. She worries about my social life.)

Every year people come from miles around for
the parade, not to mention the barbecued chicken
that we consider a traditional St. Patrick's Day entrée. Folks seem to enjoy watching the Shriners
turn circles on their Harleys and balloon-bearing
clowns scare the crap out of innocent children
standing along the side of the road. For some people
the attraction is just the revelation of the grand
marshal. That revelation is always kept secret from
the public until the parade begins, and there's a
good profit to be made if you happen to place your
bet on the right celebrity. In years past we've had
news anchors from all the major Nashville stations,
as well as the Perky Penguin, an animated figure
who telecasts school-closing reports on snowy days.
Once we even had a minor soap opera star who'd
been conned into taking the job by his elderly
grandmother, a Jesus Creek resident.

But the suspense had waned. Hometown beauty
Glenda Richmond was the hands-down favorite for
grand marshal, because Glenda had recently won
the title of Miss Tennessee National. The morning
after her victory, gigantic signs appeared at the four
corners of town: WELCOME TO JESUS CREEK—HOME OF
MISS TENNESSEE. My guess is those signs will hang
there till they rot, because we don't have many success stories around here and we like to get our
money's worth from the few who make it big.

The alternate form of entertainment for the local
gamblers was the statue. Roger Shelton, one of our
more colorful residents, was head of the committee
to install a new statue in the leprechaun-size park
down at the end of Morning Glory Way. In my opinion he'd come up with a darned good idea. Anyone
who wanted to cast a vote for the local hero to be
immortalized in stone had only to buy a ballot for
five dollars. Those smitten with self-interest, as well

as the many historians who've chosen personal idols
among the dead, had bought lots of ballots. It may
not have been fair, but it was a clever way to fi-
nance the project.

Roger had never shown much interest in community projects before, and I, for one, wondered
what sort of trouble he was cooking up now. Not
that I'm a suspicious woman. I just know Roger,
and creating havoc is his primary reason for living.

Apparently no one else had noticed that about
him, or maybe they were willing to overlook it for
the time being, because folks sure were being
mighty friendly to him. Possibly because Roger was
the only person who knew which hero had won the
bizarre balloting. And he wasn't talking. Those who
gave a damn had been trying to guess who the win-
ner might be, much as they'd previously speculated
about the identity of the grand marshal.

By mid-February, though, the locals had dropped
even that riveting subject in favor of something
more gruesome. Police in a neighboring county had
just found the mutilated body of a young woman.
She was the third victim of a killer the papers had
started calling the Night Terror. I don't know why
in hell reporters want to give colorful names to people like that. It makes them sound like cartoon
superheroes, when they're actually soulless demons
from beyond the depths of hell.

The latest victim, Kimberly Dawn Tucker, had
been a saint. Her teachers had adored her, and her
neighbors owed her their eternal gratitude for the
many kind acts she'd rendered. She'd been an honor
roll student and a humanitarian. The only reason
Kimberly Dawn had not already received the Nobel
Peace Prize was because she had postponed college
in order to support her aged mother and commune
with unicorns.

So the news reports implied. Still, I couldn't help feel that Kimberly Dawn's intelligence had waned when she hopped into that car with her killer.

Forgive my sarcasm. I'm sure Kimberly Dawn was a fine young woman who would have made a far greater contribution to the world than the Night Terror ever will. But even if she'd been a complete waste of oxygen, she had a right to life, and some maniac had stolen that from her. I hoped he'd fry.

Anyway, the reason this death caused so much excitement in our community was because it seemed to establish a pattern. Each of the three victims had been killed cleanly and quickly, the papers said, but the police were withholding forensic details until an arrest was made. The first two deaths had occurred farther east, toward Nashville. We accept, maybe even expect, uncivilized behavior in faraway cities, and none of us paid much attention to the initial reports. But a squad of professionals had determined from the latest death that the killer was following a pattern—and they felt his fourth victim was likely to be found in or near Jesus Creek.

Women who lived alone were being cautioned to stay home after dark, with their windows and doors locked. If they had to go out—well, it was the usual warning. The one that potential victims always ignore, thus becoming actual victims. I read about it in the Benton Harbor newspaper and wished again, for about the thousandth time, that *The Jesus Creek Headlight* hadn't burned down last winter. For one thing, that's where I used to work. The pay wasn't much, but it was considerably better than the salary I made waiting tables at Eloise's. For another, I'd have had access to more information as a newspaper employee. You'd be surprised what people will tell you if they think you're press.

An outsider wandering into Jesus Creek would not believe that it's normally a quiet town. In addition to the flurry of activity surrounding the St. Pat preparations, county police had taken to patrolling the streets. And even the local four-man police force had beefed up its patrols, with each man taking an extra shift every other day. Not one of them would admit that the precautions were because of the Night Terror, but if you know our local cops at all, you'd have no trouble figuring out that something big must be in the works to get *them* on the streets with that much dedication.

Some of us suspected that actual FBI agents were lurking in the shrubbery, although this had been confirmed only by Frankie Mae Weathers's report of a shadowy figure she'd seen outside the courthouse late one night. No explanation for why Frankie Mae was in the vicinity, by the way. And Reb Gassler, the police chief, had told us that Jesus Creek was just another speck on the map until a crime actually occurred, and therefore unlikely to draw hordes of law enforcement at this premature date.

At any rate, I had more immediate concerns on Monday morning. It's always the same at Eloise's. Benny and Chester come in, sit at their regular table by the door, and order their standard breakfasts. I don't even bother to give them menus anymore.

Then the folks who work at the paper mill over in Benton Harbor start to pour in, but mostly they order sausage and biscuits to go. About seven-thirty or eight o'clock, the other store owners come in, but they've usually eaten breakfast at home. They just drop by Eloise's for a friendly cup of coffee. The first few days I worked there, it nearly drove me nuts. Say four men would come in, sit at the one large table in the middle of the room, and each would have a cup of coffee. Then two more people would come in, sit at the same table, and have coffee. Then three would leave, but another one would come in. Half the time I couldn't tell who'd ordered, who'd paid, who'd left, or who was in the john.

Finally Eloise convinced me not to worry about it. She said everyone would leave money on the table, and by golly, she was right. We'd count the used cups on the table, and if the cups outweighed the money, the last coffee drinker would make up the difference. And if I found more change than was necessary, I called the difference a tip and kept it.

So on Monday I was running around with a coffeepot in one hand and an order pad in the other, just like always, while the radio on the shelf above the glasses played a bouncy country tune. Eloise used to have a jukebox, but no one ever bothered to put money in it. Eloise moved it out and now she just keeps the dial set to an all-country station on her little AM portable.

The weather was still chilly in the early part of the morning, so people were wearing jackets and hats when they arrived for breakfast. That's one reason the new guy stood out like he did. He was wearing jeans and a T-shirt, no coat. I caught him from the corner of my eye when he first walked in. He looked the place over quickly, maybe checking to see if he knew anyone, then he settled on a counter stool.

"Hi there," I said in my best we're-here-to-serve-you voice. "Like to see a menu?"

He looked at me, but he didn't smile the way most customers do. "Yes, ma'am," he said.

While he considered the breakfast possibilities, I poured a cup of coffee and set it on the counter in front of him. The other customers were surreptitiously studying him. We have our share of eccentrics in Jesus Creek, but they're *quietly* peculiar. This man had a beard and a ponytail, which singled him out for attention right away. But it was the earring—a dangling cross with a tiny diamond—that worried me. We do have a few narrow-minded rednecks in town, and I thought the man's jewelry might be more than they could handle without comment.

Either I'd underestimated them or they decided it was too early in the morning for confrontation, because by the time the stranger was ready to order, everyone else in the place had gone back to coffee and conversation.

"Sausage, two over easy, catheads, and sawmill gravy," he said, and tucked the menu into the side of the napkin holder. "And a large milk, please."

I flashed him a down-home smile (something I learned from Eloise—a smile and a constantly full coffee cup will get you a bigger tip) and asked, "What kind of jelly would you like? We've got grape, mixed, or apple."

"Apple."

So I reached under the counter and came up with a handful of plastic jelly packets. I couldn't quite put my finger on the guy's pulse. He wasn't being rude. In fact, he was as courteous as any customer I'd ever had. It was just that he didn't smile, or make small talk about the weather, or flirt—he didn't even mention the upcoming parade.

I kept busy arranging his paper napkin and utensils until the order was ready. Eloise had been passing the coffeepot around the room while I did that, and I'd noticed her glancing over her shoulder at the man. She looked puzzled, so I knew I'd been right about his being new. Eloise knows everybody in Jesus Creek, and if this Hell's Angel was a stranger to her, he certainly wasn't local.

Finally Eloise wiggled in behind the counter just as I set his plate in front of him. "Kay, honey. You want to make another pot of coffee? That bunch is sucking us dry."

"Sure," I said. I took the empty pot from her and turned around to start the coffee. We keep two pots going all day, plus a supply of filters set and ready to pop into the maker, because when the coffee drinkers get started, there's just no time to run into the back room for supplies.

Eloise gave a loud, weary sigh. "Don't ya just hate Monday?" she asked, and I assumed she was talking to the man at the counter.

"Monday's my Saturday," he said. "Don't mind it at all."

Aha. If Monday was his first day off, then he probably worked at a factory with a swing shift. Since we don't have any factories in Jesus Creek, he was obviously employed elsewhere. But then that applies to many residents here, so I didn't learn much from my swift deduction.

"You must work over at the paper mill," Eloise went on. "My cousin's been there about fifteen years now. Bill Jackson."

I turned around in time to see the guy nod. "Yeah, I know Bill. We worked the same shift until about three months ago."

"Bill's a card, idn' he? I missed your name, though."

"Wayne Holland," he said, and sat up straighter, as if he'd been reprimanded for poor manners and was trying to atone for it.

"Well, hi there, Wayne." When Eloise starts this kind of chatter with a man, she sounds just like

Dolly Parton. In fact, she looks a little like Dolly, too, what with her blonde hair and full figure. "Now you can't be from around here. I'd know you, or at least know *of* you."

"No, ma'am," Wayne said. "But I'm about to be. I'm over here today looking for a place to rent. I've got an appointment to see a place this morning, on Main Street."

"That'd be Roger Shelton's old apartment. Well, I sure hope you like it. If you don't—hey, Kay. Are you still trying to rent that room of yours?"

"No," I said quickly. What was the matter with her? A serial killer was stalking women in our area, and she was trying to set me up with a complete stranger. "I rented that a few months ago. Remember?" Of course she remembered. She's always giving free meals to my tenant.

"Oh, well." Eloise waved one hand to indicate that it wasn't important anyway. "You'll probably like Roger's apartment."

About then Benny and Chester signaled for more coffee, and that set the whole bunch off, so I spent the next fifteen minutes refilling cups. I didn't get back to the counter until Wayne Holland was pushing his money and ticket toward Eloise. "Nice to meet you," he told her as he eased off the stool. "And the breakfast was great. If I do wind up living in Jesus Creek, I know where I'll do my eating."

Now most men would have winked while delivering that line. Eloise inspires come-ons, subtle and otherwise. And the fact that Wayne Holland was probably fifteen or twenty years younger than her shouldn't have stopped him. But he just went on out the door with that same serious expression on his face, the one he'd worn the whole time he'd been there.

As soon as he was gone, I leaned over to Eloise and whispered, "Don't invite strange men to rent my room. Don't you know there's a nut running loose around here? It could be him for all we know."

She just laughed. "I know men, sugar. I was trying to improve your life. This one could be just right for you."

For a minute I was actually speechless. The last three or four she'd tried to fix me up with had also been just right, according to Eloise. I can't seem to make her understand that I'm in no condition to get involved in a relationship just now. One of the things I've learned in the twelve-step program I attend is that, until I get myself together, I'm almost certain to pick another man just like the one I was involved with last time. The one who lied so smoothly, swept me off my feet with his vulnerability, and then stole half my worldly goods to support his chemical habit.

Even more disturbing was Eloise's track record. Aside from the fact that she's had four husbands of her own, not one of the couples she's thrown together has lived happily ever after. Even if I'd been interested in Wayne Holland, Eloise's confidence in the match would have changed my mind.

"Now, Kay. You're already twenty-five and you don't even have a boyfriend! Don't look at me like that. Didn't you think he was cute?"

"For God's sake, Eloise! He was wearing an earring. He's probably a professional knee buster."

"That last man of yours looked like Beaver Cleaver's big brother, too. You can't tell by the clothes they wear, sugar. It takes experience, and I've got it. Maybe this Wayne Holland is just the one you've been looking for."

"And maybe I've got a live chicken in my

pocket," I said, shoving another filter full of Maxwell House in the coffee maker.

Eloise raised her eyebrows. "Better watch where it pecks."

CHAPTER
2

The Magician: Travel with power, but direct it wisely.

WHEN I GOT HOME THAT AFTERNOON there was a motorcycle parked in front of the house, just behind John's old Ford. John is my roommate of two months. I met him over in Benton Harbor at the twelve-step program we're both involved with. John is a recovering alcoholic and drug abuser—ten years substance-free. And I'm recovering from a long and sordid relationship with a nonrecovering drug abuser. So there I was, putting my note about an available room on the bulletin board, when John Patrick Sullivan stepped up with his own note about needing a place to rent.

We had coffee for four hours in a dingy café (John replaced his illegal addictions with caffeine), agreed to give the arrangement six months, and the next day he moved into my spare room. The house isn't much—just a two-bedroom frame with bad plumbing—but John is tidy and neither of us owns much, so it works out. I bought the house more for convenience than beauty. It's on Morning Glory Way, right beside Proctor's Gas Station, near the old newspaper office and catty-corner to Eloise's. Of course, when I became a homeowner I had no idea I'd be working for below minimum wage and tips, but I'd gotten the loan through Farmers, so when *The Headlight* burned and my income decreased, so did the payments. Just not enough to make life comfortable.

My car died a week after *The Headlight* did. Naturally, with the house payment and sudden unemployment, I couldn't afford new transportation. But John has an old Ford with bald tires and well over a hundred thousand miles on the odometer. He lets me borrow it whenever I need to go out of town.

John explained that he was a counselor at the consolidated high school here. That seemed like a trustworthy reference to me. I figured counselors have to be reasonably sane, even counselors who haven't quite finished their degrees and are called on to teach math three hours a day as well. (It's a small, unassuming school.)

Even though I'd never seen him in action, and I didn't know any high school students to ask, I figured John probably did a great job. He's tall and dark and wears a beard to cover a scar that he claims he picked up in his gang days. I'll bet the girls love it. And since he was the ultimate bad boy in his youth, he said he could relate to the troublemakers he counseled.

"No matter how rotten their lives are," he told me once, "I can make them feel better about it. I can always top their stories with my own."

So I wasn't surprised to find John sitting at the rusty table on our screened-in front porch, a scruffy-looking teenage boy with him. John's tarot cards were arranged on the table between them. I glanced at the cards just long enough to notice that the spread held an unusually large amount of swords.

John uses the cards a lot—carries them in his pocket everywhere he goes, in fact. I don't know if he really believes they reveal the future, but that's not why he uses them anyway. He says he picks up on the questioner's thoughts by reading the person, then translates what he sees into a tarot reading. After that he watches his subject for reactions, and from this, or so he claims, he's able to determine the real problem that his student is dealing with.

John looked up and gave me a nod. The kid just stared at me.

"This is Kay," John said to the boy. "And this is Scott."

I gave Scott my grownup-to-adolescent smile. "Hi. How's it going?"

Scott muttered a greeting and continued to stare through me. My mother would have pegged him as white trash, but I hesitated to do so. The fact that he wore ragged, dirty jeans and a sweatshirt with the obscene name of a rap group on it could simply mean that he was fashionable. His surly attitude might have been an indication that he lacked parental guidance, or it could be a symptom of raging teenage hormones. Although I personally was never surly, even at my worst stage of development. I'm codependent. I *always* wanted people to like me.

"I'll just get out of your way," I said to John. "You go right ahead with your reading. I have to get ready for tonight anyway. Y'all enjoy yourselves." And before young Scott could sneer at my cheerful banter, I went into the house.

The cat met me just inside the door and rubbed her fluffy little head against my leg. It wasn't me she adored. It was the alluring scent of hamburger on my clothes. After working in the diner all day I inevitably came home smelling like sweat and old grease. So the first order of business was a bath, a long hot one. And on evenings when I moonlight, I always use every product in the Lady Mystique line, so it takes twice as long to finish.

Those parties are one of the ways I make ends meet. I'm a beauty consultant for Lady Mystique cosmetics and skin care products. That means I sell the stuff during in-home demonstrations, much like Tupperware parties. I also baby-sit, walk dogs, mow yards, and every now and then I pick up a few dollars from a poetry contest.

I tried to scoop Bella (short for Belladonna) up in my arms, but she ran her claws across my hand and marched off into the kitchen. No doubt to relieve herself, since the litter box was in the bathroom. I'd picked up the cat when she was just a scrawny stray kitten, optimistically envisioning quiet evenings at home with my devoted feline companion to keep me company. And Bella had repaid my kind act by drawing blood almost every day since, repeatedly turning up her nose at the expensive delicacies I'd tried to feed her, and practicing her excremental habits in any room in which there was not a litter box. I made a mental note to search later for whatever little gift she'd left for me, then locked myself in the bathroom for a peaceful soak. Bella started scratching at the door as soon as I was wet. I decided to ignore her.

By the time I came out of the bathroom in my slip, my hair wrapped in a towel, and half a pound of makeup on my face, John was stretched out on the couch, watching a news special about the Night Terror and eating a bologna sandwich. (That's pronounced *baloney* around here, also known as poor man's steak.) He'd made a pot of coffee, but there was only a little left.

"Is Scott one of your kids from school?"

"Uh-hum," John said. "Screwed up bad, too. But he's finally started to open up. Of course, I could have told you the story anyway. Mom's live-ins change every couple of weeks. Dad's a boozer and physically abusive to boot. Scott has two younger sisters, both of whom were probably sexually abused by Dad before he left. Maybe Scott was, too. He's the most hostile kid I've met so far." John shook his head, which meant: it's a damned shame, but what can you do?

"Scott told you this?" I felt my stomach tighten at the thought of hearing a confession like that.

"Of course he didn't tell me. Scott would perceive that as vulnerability, and it's extremely important for him to present a show of personal force. But I know."

John does this. Often. If he had any objectivity, he'd admit that he's projecting his own childhood traumas. For weeks now he's been trying to dig information out of me about the abuse I suffered by any or all of my male relatives. He simply will not believe that I had a normal life. Knowing this, I decided to delay my opinion of Scott's father for a while. Even if Scott and his sisters hadn't suffered sexual abuse, it was clear that Scott came from a broken and unhappy family.

"I don't know how you work with these people. Not the regular ones," I explained. "I don't mean the ones whose biggest problem is breaking up with the boyfriend or trying to decide on a college. But the kids like Scott. Doesn't it break your heart?"

"Of course. Scott's just like me. But I didn't have a counselor who tried to help me understand that my problems stemmed from exposure to a dysfunctional background, and that I was not responsible. Nobody cared whether I survived or not. I may be the only friend this boy ever had. The other students can't stand him, and I can see why. He's scared and hurting, but he's too young to admit it. So he covers up. He swears at the teachers, which gets him expelled about twice a month. He beats up the other boys and makes lewd remarks to the girls. He tears up books and equipment. He steals from the lockers."

"A real sweetheart. Wouldn't we all be better off if you just drowned him now?"

John gave me one of his sighs. To remind me that I was being insensitive and impractical. And to make me feel guilty about having a regular set of parents. "Drowning him won't fix the problem. If I can get Scott to see that none of this is his fault, just maybe he'll be able to climb out of the hellhole he's in. He needs to find an area of control, anything at all that he has power over."

"Of course you're right." Already I felt guilty about that drowning comment. With all that young Scott had been exposed to, it was no wonder he felt angry and betrayed. I resolved to treat him with extra kindness and consideration the next time we met. "I admire your patience and your desire to help the boy," I said to John. "But honestly, what are the chances that you'll straighten him out?"

"Absolutely zero. He'll have to straighten himself out. The only purpose I serve is to show him the possibilities. Kay, he has no concept—none—of normal life. He doesn't realize there are constructive ways to retake control of his life. Convincing him of that is like telling a blind man to look before he crosses the street."

"If Scott doesn't even understand what you're talking about, then how are you going to help him?"

"By filling him in on my life story," John said simply.

"Oh boy." I'd heard that story. It had taken three days for John to divulge just the most relevant events. I've been getting details ever since.

"I've told him all about my childhood. He sees the parallel. By now he's started to identify with me, so when I explain how I pulled myself out of the pit, he should realize that he can do it, too."

"But if he's never known anything in his life except abuse and—"

"That helps. He's seen the very worst of it. The good will look even better to him. There's a balance in everything. You can't experience love until you've felt hatred. You can't be entirely happy until you've been completely miserable." John slugged down the last of his coffee. "You need a little deception—to recognize truth."

"Right," I said abruptly. John talks a lot. I'd always thought counselors were supposed to listen, but when he's not in his shrink mode, he pontificates. Fast and nonstop. "I've got a show tonight," I reminded him.

"I know." He looked me over carefully, implying what he'd said many times in the past—that I would develop personality problems if I didn't stop playing two different roles.

You see, before I became a beauty consultant, I never even owned mascara. Now half the time I'd pass for a professional model. The other half, when I'm being my real self, I look like a dirt farmer's wife caught, with no hope of rescue, in the Great Depression.

"You need the car?" he offered, after making his point.

"No," I said, digging in the front closet for my black pumps. "I'm only going to Pamela Satterfield's. But I will need the typewriter to fill out a report afterward. Anything new on the Night Terror?" I pointed to the television with my shoe.

"I'll leave the typewriter on the kitchen table," John said. "The police are stumped. One true-crime expert has urged us to remain calm, since, according to him, the murders are not necessarily related. Apparently he covers the subject in great depth in his new book, which he'll be signing at an area bookstore tomorrow. Another expert tells us there's a maniac on the prowl and we'd better bolt our doors if we don't want to become statistics. People are buying guns."

"Terrific. A bunch of nervous maidens stalking their backyards with Uzis. That's a damned good reason to stay home at night."

"You know where the gun is?"

I nodded. John had brought the little gun with him when he moved in, then insisted on keeping it behind the towels in the bathroom closet. Once he explained to me how the nasty thing was supposed to work, but I'd managed to avoid actually firing it. He said the recoil would probably knock me down, but any intruder with good sense would be gone by then anyway. It's not the people with good sense I worry about.

"Every now and then I check to be sure it's still there. And to be sure I haven't forgotten where the safety is or where the trigger is—"

"Safety?" John looked up from the television.

"That little button on the side."

"Kay," John said, with just a touch of superiority, "that isn't a safety. It opens the chamber."

"Oh, well," I said, with little concern, "a peashooter like that won't help anyway. It probably wouldn't even make a dent in a burglar."

John took a deep breath and tried hard not to

laugh. "That particular peashooter is what we call a .357 Magnum. Trust me, it will make a dent."

"Oh," I said. I'd heard of a .357, of course. Isn't that what Dirty Harry uses? But I'd always pictured it as a large weapon. I still thought John was wrong about it scaring off an intruder, though. Suppose the criminal didn't know any more about Magnums than I did.

CHAPTER
3

The High Priestess, reversed: You have failed to follow your natural highway. Trust intuition to lead you.

PAMELA SATTERFIELD IS THE ASSISTANT LIbrarian at the Jesus Creek Public Library. She's the last person I'd have expected to hold a makeup party. Pamela is—well, I guess I'd have to say conservative. She dresses well, but not too flashy. Or maybe I've just gotten used to Eloise's fashion sense. Pamela's hair is always neatly groomed, just a bit out of date. And she's been wearing that same blue eyeshadow since Nixon went to China, but I intended to fix that right quick.

The hostess, you see, gets a free makeover as one of her incentive gifts. And then I do a makeover for one of the guests, while the others watch and supposedly learn. The only worry I had was whether or not Pamela would allow me to strip her face down to bare skin. Some women don't want anyone to see them completely devoid of makeup.

Pamela had mellowed lately, though. She used to

bitch like she had a license for it, but all of a sudden, she turned happy as a cow chewing cud, even around mere acquaintances. Once she had lunch in the diner and left me a tip. Personally, I think it has something to do with German Hunt, the deputy police chief. German is a redneck with pretensions. A few months ago he developed a crush on Pamela. When he first started hanging around the library, I half expected Pamela to rip him to shreds, but darned if he didn't win her over.

For the last month I've seen them having dinner in Eloise's about once or twice a week. I wouldn't say that Pamela has turned into a simpering fool, but she manages to look like a woman infatuated while retaining her dignity. And German? Lord, he's even stopped chewing tobacco because she asked him to. That's probably been as hard for him as giving up alcohol was for John.

Pamela met me at her front door (absolutely no one uses her back door—she isn't that mellow) dressed in a rosy pink skirt and matching sweater. She knits them herself. Her hair was teased up as usual, and she was wearing that peacock eyeshadow, just as I'd predicted.

"Hello, Kay," she said smoothly. "Come on in. I've just about got everything ready."

I followed her into the spotless living room and set my display case on the floor beside the card table she had set up in front of her picture window. According to the Lady Mystique training manual, we beauty consultants are supposed to supply our own card tables. But that's not practical in my case. I usually walk to my parties, and it's trouble enough lugging around that suitcase full of demo products. Besides, none of my hostesses have ever read the training manual.

"Pamela, I'd like to thank you for letting me

come into your home tonight." We're required to
say that. "And I hope—"

"I get a twenty-five percent discount for hosting
the party, right?" Pamela interrupted.

"Well, yes. And a complimentary makeover as
well."

"Let's do it, then," she said, and plopped down in
the folding chair beside the card table. "And don't
dawdle. I've got the hotline tonight, and I want everyone out by ten."

Pamela is a dedicated volunteer with the
domestic-abuse prevention group in our county.

By the time I'd taught Pamela the art of shad-
owing and defining, her other guests had started to
arrive. They were all local, women I've known all
my life, and I had to keep reminding myself that I
was the professional. Ordinarily when I'm demonstrating, I'd rather play to a room full of hostile
strangers than face friends.

One look at the refreshments Pamela had prepared—Ritz crackers and peanut butter—told me
that the evening would not be a rip-roaring success.
Atmosphere is important, and while I don't encourage my hostesses to have these parties catered, I do
hope to see a little enthusiasm and concern for the
guests' enjoyment.

Sarah Elizabeth Leach, head librarian and Pamela's boss, squirmed through the entire program,
though I could hardly blame her. In the fifth month
of pregnancy, she'd already gained thirty pounds
and looked as if she might be harboring a family of
sharecroppers under that maternity smock.

As if she didn't have enough trouble, her mother-
in-law, Eliza, insisted on sitting right beside her
and stuffing pillows behind Sarah Elizabeth's back
every time the girl looked as if she'd found a tol-
erable position.

Delia Cannon, always discreet, had sidled up to me just before the demonstration began. Were my products cruelty-free? she wanted to know. In research or in manufacture of the Lady Mystique line, had any animals been abused? I assured her that the company had applied for a listing with PETA, but Delia didn't seem overly trusting and plucked up a jar of moisturizer to study the ingredients while I ran through my opening spiel.

Clara Maddox was there, too, questioning every word out of my mouth. Were our products really of the highest quality? Wasn't it true that all cosmetics are made from the same ingredients? She'd heard that dermatologists recommended plain soap and water for a lovely complexion, and not layers of expensive creams.

Clara's husband is an attorney. He runs a one-man law office on Main Street and he's got a pretty respectable income. Clara wears exquisite jewelry and fine-quality clothes. Too bad she has no taste. And she talks too much.

I could see I had my work cut out for me—so I leapt into the fray. I've found that these audiences love slapstick, so once I'd selected my model and stripped off her makeup with Lady Mystique Gentle Cleanser, I asked her to suck in her cheeks. The room was with me. They chuckled and pointed at the model. And for a moment there, I thought I really had them.

Then Clara started talking about the Night Terror and the latest theories devised by the Tennessee Bureau of Investigation. "Devereaux"—that's her husband—"talked to a TBI agent just this morning, and he said they've got the next murder site pinpointed. He says it's definitely going to be in Jesus Creek, because the killer is moving almost exactly fifty miles for each murder, and he's going in a straight line."

Thank you, Clara, I thought, for enlightening us all.

"The TBI man also says the Night Terror is killing blondes with blue eyes, probably because they remind him of his mother."

"Have they caught him?" I asked.

"No, honey," Clara said with surprise. "Didn't you hear what I just said?"

"Then how do they know what his mother looks like?"

"It's a psychological profile. They always do that for serial killers. Why, there are experts who can tell just about everything about a person from the clues he leaves behind."

"Clues?" asked Delia Cannon, who'd been transfixed by my demonstration until then. "What clues?"

Clara decided to turn coy. "Oh, Delia. You know I can't discuss that. The police are holding back some evidence so they can weed out the professional confessors. You know every time there's an unsolved murder, just hundreds of people come forward and claim they've done it. But none of them ever *have* done it, so the police ask questions about things that only the killer could know."

"Yes," Delia said, with more patience than I could have mustered. "But as I understand it, this killer has been particularly careful not to leave clues."

"There's the weapon," Eliza pointed out.

According to news reports, the Night Terror had used the same knife on all his victims. But if he didn't leave it behind, I couldn't see how it qualified as evidence.

"And the similarity of setting," Delia added.

"Each victim has been found in a secluded, grassy area, such as a park or refuge."

"I can't imagine why you insist on speculating about this psychopath," Pamela said haughtily. "It's a disgusting subject."

Well, I agreed with her, but that didn't stop the flow of conversation for a minute.

"How accurately can they pinpoint a weapon?" Delia asked. "Did Devereaux speak with one of the experts, or just an agent passing through? You know, spreading rumors could damage efforts to catch the killer. It's facts we need, Clara. Otherwise the vigilantes will be lynching anyone with a facial tic or a peculiar name."

"Right," Clara agreed, desperately trying to bring attention back to herself. "But the police have given us as much information as they can. We know the killer uses a knife, and that he transports the bodies in a vehicle of some kind. Of course, they're not describing the nature of the mutilation, but as I've said, I can't discuss that. You know what concerns me? It's been almost a week since the last murder. That was on the twentieth, right? Up to now, he's killed someone every ten days, so he must be feeling the urge."

"You think this comes in cycles?" I asked. "Like a hormone shift?" I admit it. I was being nasty.

Clara nodded. "Same as a wild animal that gets a taste for blood, don't you think? So by now, every blonde woman in Jesus Creek is in danger. Doesn't that terrify you?"

"No." I figured I'd better say something if I was going to retake control of the evening. "If he's only killing blondes, I have nothing to worry about. As for those of you who qualify, I can recommend Lady Mystique Hair Color, number 366, Bashful Brunette. Now if you extend the eyeliner beyond this center point, you're going to look like an Oriental raccoon. So remember to stop—"

"Excuse me," Delia said, holding up the jar of moisturizer she'd been examining, "but what, exactly, is hydrolyzed animal protein?"

Well, after that the evening was shot. My model couldn't keep quiet long enough for me to apply the lipstick properly. Pamela started bustling around and tidying up long before I was finished, and the whole crowd huddled around Clara to pump her for that vital information she'd insisted she couldn't reveal. Too damn bad, I thought, that Clara isn't a blonde.

As it turned out, Pamela did well. Her guests were so caught up in conversation that they ordered a ton of products without thinking. (Except for Delia, who apologized to me for disrupting my show; even so, she explained she was less than enthusiastic about applying Lady Mystique products to her skin.) Pamela got a percentage of the total sales in merchandise. It took me nearly an hour to calculate our profits, and by that time everyone else had gone home.

So there I was, traipsing down the sidewalk late at night with nothing but a Lady Mystique suitcase for protection. As I've mentioned, I wasn't overly concerned about the killer coming my way, because I'm not a blonde and I don't have blue eyes. And to think all these years I've regretted my coloring.

Still, with the town shut down for the night and only the sound of an early spring wind for company, I was getting edgy. I tried to walk briskly and with a purposeful stride, but that isn't easy when you're in heels and lugging a twenty-pound suitcase.

By the time I reached the house, I was panting in a most unladylike way. Probably from sheer terror. I hurried inside the porch enclosure and started digging through my purse for the door key. I'd already seen that John's car wasn't parked out front, and of course, I hadn't expected him to be there. John attends twelve-step meetings as often as five times a week. It's another of his addictions.

Sometimes when I return home from a party he's already there, but once in a while—when he hits a meeting several miles away—I get there first. It would be easier for everyone if Benton Harbor or Jesus Creek held meetings every night. Neither town is big enough for that, so John has to travel all over the countryside in search of support groups.

I used to attend those meetings pretty regularly myself. Lately I've missed a lot, largely because I'm working two jobs and just don't have time. John says that if I really wanted to go I'd make the time, and I guess he's right. He says I should give some thought to that—*why* am I skipping meetings? John likes to know the why of things.

I unlocked the front door and entered a chilly, gloomy house. In an effort to conserve energy, not to mention money, John had turned down the heat before he left. I dumped the suitcase in the front closet, kicked off my shoes, and adjusted the thermostat. Then I turned on my electric blanket and changed into a fuzzy bathrobe and thick socks. Bella hadn't returned from her nightly hunt, so I had the house entirely to myself for a change.

It was almost ten-thirty, and I had to be at work before six the next morning; but I wanted to catch the news before I went to sleep, so I flicked on the television. Cable hasn't made its way to Jesus Creek, so my options were limited. I endured a deadly-dull talk show because I knew that if the Night Terror had been active, I could count on a newsbreak. I felt confident that the killer was al-

ready tucked into his bed for the night. As Clara
had pointed out, his pattern had left us with a victim once every ten days. It had been only five days
since the last attack. A nagging little voice reminded me that he wasn't necessarily keeping track
on his calendar. For my own peace of mind, I decided to pretend that the pattern was important to
the Night Terror and that he wouldn't break it now.

I heard John's car pull up just as the perky star-
let began her patter about her new, gritty movie
and the acting challenge it provided. (Translation:
she didn't wear noticeable makeup for this one.)

I switched off the set and opened the door for
John, mightily relieved to have him home again. I
hope feminists won't revoke my membership in
world sisterhood, but I felt safer knowing there was
a big, strong man in the house.

"Party go okay?" he asked as he came in.

"Usual. Clara Maddox was there."

John grinned. He knows Clara. "Do you know
they've already erected that statue in the park—the
one commissioned by the Historical Society?"

"The one commissioned by Roger Shelton, you
mean. No, I had no idea it had been set up." I was
surprised that Roger had allowed it to be delivered
so soon. "What does it look like?"

"It's a tall lump, covered with a tarp. Very phal-
lic. And two guys with sticks on their shoulders are
standing guard." John took off his jacket and hung
it neatly in the closet. "I guess Roger's serious
about keeping the secret. His childhood must have
been one phenomenal exercise in torment."

"Oh, John. You think everyone had a tormented
childhood. Roger's just trying to add to the St. Patrick's Day atmosphere." Actually, I agreed with
John. Roger's warped sense of humor probably does
stem from some sort of emotional trauma. Still, I

like Roger, and I didn't want to give John any excuse to start psychoanalyzing him.

"Everyone *does* have a tormented childhood. We healthy individuals make peace with the inner child. Some people, on the other hand, block it out for years, but it keeps coming back to get them. Nightmares."

"Nightmares?"

"Uh-huh. Subconscious alerting you to sit up and pay attention. Had any nightmares lately, Kay?" John gave me his probing would-you-like-to-talk-about-it? look.

"Just the one about being naked in a room full of people."

"Tell me more." This time he leered. "Describe it in detail." John likes to pretend that he's in lust with me. Truth is, if I ever so much as batted my lashes at him, he'd probably drop from fright.

Before I could think of something sick enough to please him, Bella crawled in through her cat door and dumped a morsel of mouse at John's feet. Then she headed down the hall, no doubt to insure herself a good night's sleep in the middle of my bed.

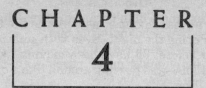

CHAPTER
4

The Empress, reversed: You are expending energy on unprofitable side trips.

ALL NIGHT I'D DREAMED OF HOMICIDAL MA-niacs, waking briefly between the variations of murder to toss and turn and listen for strange sounds at my window. By the time the alarm clock announced the arrival of Tuesday morning, I'd had a total of two hours' sleep.

When I stumbled into work, Eloise had the radio blaring Willie Nelson. A guaranteed waker-upper.

"You had a hell of a night, I'll bet," Eloise said, after a quick glance at my swollen, pasty face. She, of course, was bright and chipper and could have been the ad model for megavitamin supplements.

"Makeup demo at Pam Satterfield's," I explained. "The party ran late, and then I wound up listening to John until one A.M." I stashed my jacket and purse under the counter and started the first pot of coffee for the day.

Before the customers start pouring in, the diner

is a dim, airless chamber, as if all the life is sucked
out of it during the night. Even with sufficient sleep
the night before, I'd have been moving like molas-
ses. But Eloise was buzzing around like a queen bee
on a deadline.

"Sell a lot?" she asked over her shoulder. Her
arms were full of napkin holders, which she'd col-
lected and brought to the counter for refilling. She
and the cook had already peeled vegetables and had
them steaming, stewing, and frying in preparation
for the lunch rush.

Fortunately, we waitresses aren't responsible for
anything more than waiting tables and minimal
maintenance of facilities. I was already having
trouble fitting the coffee filters into the machine.
Anything more difficult would be completely beyond me until I got a good night's sleep or a mas-
sive dose of caffeine.

"Yes, as a matter of fact," I answered. "I *did* sell
a lot. But halfway through my presentation Clara
Maddox started carrying on about the Night Terror
and nobody paid any attention to me. I swear, if I
hear another word about that sicko killer—" Just
then—with improbably perfect timing—the radio
bleated forth with the station's emergency-bulletin
pulse beat.

The disc jockey–news reader began his report.
"This just in. State police report that a Laytonville
woman had a narrow escape last night."

Eloise and I both stopped our chores and looked
at each other. There was dead silence from the radio, and for a second I thought the station had gone
off the air. But it was just the deejay taking a dramatic pause.

He continued: "Twenty-seven-year-old Cathy Ann
Hopkins reported to police late last night that she
had been held captive for approximately two hours

by an unidentified man before she managed to escape. She had apparently been accosted near Laytonville, a town located seventy-five miles southeast of Nashville. Police say the young woman jumped from her abductor's moving car as it slowed for a turn. Hopkins then ran into a nearby convenience store and asked employees there to notify authorities. Police have not confirmed rumors that this was another Night Terror attack."

Eloise sighed audibly. "Guess Jesus Creek made it through another one," she said. "And I guess those experts will have to get their heads together again. Poor girl. Must have been scared silly."

I nodded, exhausted and relieved. I called up my mental map of the county. It was sketchy, but sufficient to tell me that Laytonville is far, far away from our peaceful hamlet. Since Jesus Creek is almost directly west of Nashville, and since the Night Terror had previously been moving in a direct east-to-west line, it was obvious he had changed course. He'd decided Jesus Creek wasn't worth bothering with. Or maybe he'd never intended to invade our fair community anyway. Of course, this latest incident wasn't necessarily the work of the Night Terror, but I sure wanted to believe it was.

The news bulletin continued for a couple of minutes, and then, in a sort of tribute to the Higher Power that had saved Cathy Hopkins's life, the deejay played "Amazing Grace." Just as Judy Collins sang the final note, our first customers entered.

Benny and Chester made themselves comfortable at their regular table by the door while I poured their coffee and gave the cook their order. Eloise took care of the third customer.

"Why, good morning, Wayne," Eloise called. "Fix you up with a cup?"

"Yeah," he said, and sat down at the counter.

"And a couple of fried eggs with sausage and biscuits."

I poured his coffee and set it in front of him.
"Would you like a large milk, too?" I asked. I didn't
mean to sound sarcastic, but even I could hear it in
my voice. For some reason I couldn't put my finger
on, just being in the same room with Wayne Holland set me off. His presence made me jittery, the
way I'd always felt when Gary came home too
happy or too depressed—an unmistakable sign that
he was controlled by chemicals. Wayne seemed to
be a nice enough man (as that gender goes), but I
wasn't getting that edgy feeling for nothing.

"Good memory," he said. "Yeah, milk."

"How'd the apartment look to you?" Eloise asked.
She was dashing around the room, placing replen-
ished napkin holders on the tables.

"I'm moving in this morning. Gotta start back to
work on graveyards tomorrow night, so I'll have to
get finished today."

Eloise came over to the counter and sat down on
the stool next to him. "Midnights are rough. My
first husband was on shift work. Every time he
worked nights, he'd turn into a real SOB. Come to
think of it, he was like that no matter what shift
he worked."

Wayne just shook his head, probably wondering
why any man would be a problem for Eloise.

"How long have you worked over at the Land
plant?" Land Paper Company in Benton Harbor
employs about three hundred workers, many of
them Jesus Creek residents. The pay is excellent,
and there's a waiting list a mile long. On the rare
occasion when a few jobs open up, people stand in
line half the night to apply.

"Fifteen years," Wayne said. "I started there
when it opened up, right out of high school."

"You been living in Benton Harbor all this time?" Eloise asked. "How come you decided to move to Jesus Creek now?"

"Prices are cheaper," he said. "I'm a single man again, but half the paycheck goes to my ex."

A few of our coffee drinkers had wandered in and caught the last bit of Wayne's woes. They nodded in sympathy. I almost felt sorry for him, too, but quickly reminded myself that any wife of Wayne's doubtless earned her share of that paycheck. I had to repeat that to myself a few times. Kicking the nurture habit isn't easy.

"You hear about that girl down in Laytonville?" Henry Mooten asked me as I passed around the pot. Henry had his emergency survival kit tucked between his feet. Back in November when he heard that an earthquake was predicted to hit the New Madrid fault, he'd started carrying the kit everywhere he went. Neither the fact that no one can predict earthquakes nor the fact that Jesus Creek is located more than a hundred miles from the fault had deterred Henry's preparations. And once the date of doom had passed, he decided that each subsequent day brought us closer to seismic destruction; so he continued carrying his canvas pack everywhere he went.

"Just now on the radio," I told him. "Sounds like they were wrong about Jesus Creek being in danger."

Henry sipped the steaming coffee and decided to add a little more sugar on top of the three spoons he'd already stirred in. "That's the way those experts are. Full of ideas that don't mean nothing." He was probably referring to the experts who assured us that we were not sitting on the eve of the Big One.

The rest of the table agreed with him and plunged

into a lively conversation about the examples of expert stupidity they'd witnessed. I didn't think they'd miss me, so I went back behind the counter and started up the second coffee maker, knowing we'd need it before long. Eloise was just serving Wayne his breakfast.

"Now Kay here could tell you some stories," she was saying. "She just got out of a bad relationship herself."

I groaned inwardly. The trouble with Eloise—aside from remaining deaf to my assertions that I don't *want* a guy—is that she's a hopeless romantic. She reads Barbara Cartland novels and believes them. She still has a copy of *Love Story* on her bedside table. And she truly expects Prince Charming to walk through the door of the diner and carry me away. Funny thing is, she's much more sensible when it comes to her own life. She has no illusions at all about the men *she* dates.

Wayne glanced fleetingly at me before concentrating again on his eggs and sausage. Eloise continued enumerating my virtues. She had to stretch quite a bit. Even I was impressed with my credentials as she presented them, so I decided I'd better step in and rescue Wayne before he was overcome by passion for me.

"Yeah, Wayne, I know how it is," I said, cutting off Eloise. "When you've escaped from a bad marriage, the last thing on earth you want is to get hooked up with somebody else, right? But they tell me that changes. You know what you need? Some time alone."

I could tell he wasn't sure if I was trying to save him or bury him, so I pressed on. "Take a little while to be by yourself. Don't get involved with anyone. Let it heal. You'll do just fine."

"Sounds like good advice," he said. "Is that how you handled it?"

"That's how I'm *handling* it."

Eloise had apparently gotten the hint. She piled a dozen doughnuts on a plate and carried it over to the coffee drinkers' table, leaving me alone with Wayne.

"I've had just about all I want of men," I continued. "You probably feel the same way about women."

"Well, not women in general. But my ex in particular."

"What's she like?" I asked, truly curious.

"She's a witch with a capital *b*."

Clearly he still harbored a lot of hurt and resentment. "I mean what does she look like? What does she do?"

Wayne broke open another biscuit and jellied it. "She's blonde this week," he said seriously. "Works at the bank in Benton Harbor."

Oh. That told me exactly what I wanted to know. Bank employees are conservative, well dressed, generally well mannered, and upwardly mobile. No wonder their marriage had ended. Anyone could have told them it would be a disaster. I've often thought how odd it is that the two people involved in a relationship will ignore what's perfectly obvious to the rest of the world.

Reb Gassler saved me from further conversation by bursting through the door. "Biscuits fresh?" he asked, glancing subtly at Wayne.

"No, we saved some old ones for you." Reb is always asking me silly questions. He's the local police chief, which allows—indeed, almost requires—him to ask those questions. I poured him a cup of coffee and handed him a menu. Reb is one of the few people who might order something different every morning. "Have you met Wayne here? He's just moved to town."

Reb turned to study Wayne openly, as if he hadn't been doing that all along, and stuck out his hand. "Reb Gassler," he said. "Glad to meet you. What brings you to Jesus Creek?" He flashed his good-old-boy grin—the one he uses to lull felons into a false web of security, just before he extracts full confessions from them.

Wayne went into a modified account of his relocation story while I waited patiently for Reb's breakfast order. I figured if a good look at Reb (six-feet-two, two hundred pounds of pure muscle) didn't persuade Wayne to stay out of trouble, there was no hope for him.

"Just divorced, huh?" Reb asked. "Been there myself."

"Yeah," Wayne said. "I'm still getting used to it."

"It's some hell, ain't it?"

Terrific. Reb was feeling sorry for the guy. Men always stick together, I guess, especially when they can bad-mouth the opposite sex. (I wasn't going to think about the countless times I'd heard women dragging their mates through the mud.)

"You want to eat, Reb?" I was losing patience with this newly formed men's club and wanted to get back to work.

Reb ordered pancakes, apparently unaware of my disapproval. Not that he'd have cared much if he'd noticed. Reb is the most self-contained human I've ever met. His need to win love and approval doesn't show. I've tried to get him to trust me, to understand that I'm more than willing to listen to him when he's ready to talk, but so far he still considers me a wall. That's not healthy. Bottled up hurt and anger can really take its toll, but I can't seem to

make Reb understand that. He just grins and ac-
cuses me of trying to be his mother.

While I was setting up his utensils, the conversation turned back to the Night Terror, with the
fellows at the coffee drinkers' table throwing in
their two bits. I guess Reb was relieved to learn the
latest attack had occurred outside his jurisdiction,
because he seemed a lot more relaxed than he'd
been lately. I suspected that he'd been just as anxious as the rest of us about the Night Terror's move
toward Jesus Creek. But of course, that's not something Reb would admit to.

"German wanted me to call up that psychic we
had here last summer," Reb said, in response to
Henry's question about just what the hell the police
had in mind to do next. The men at the table
laughed with him. "German's real impressed. Any
of you meet him?"

Reb had been away on vacation when deputy
chief German Hunt had turned into an admirer of
Owen Komelecki, psychic first-class. No one in the
room admitted to knowing the man, however. Probably wise.

"He's not available anyway," Eloise said, returning to the counter with the first round of dirty
coffee cups. "I talked to Kate last week and she
said they were going off to Alabama for a case."

Kate Yancy works for Komelecki, as his assistant or receptionist or whatever psychics require.
She's a Jesus Creek native. Met Komelecki while
he was in town last year, and the next any of us
knew, she'd toddled off behind him. Kate may well
be the only person who ever got out of Jesus Creek
alive, but then she keeps coming back, too. We'll
see how long her new adventure lasts.

"You mean they won't be here for the parade?"
I couldn't believe Kate would miss that. The cele-

bration also served as a sort of homecoming feast
for family and friends of Jesus Creekers, who returned to hold reunions and adorn the graves of
their departed loved ones with plastic flowers.

"Oh, they'll be here for that," Eloise assured me.
"Kate said her boss is looking forward to it. He's
never been in town for the St. Pat's parade."

"Now that this Night Terror has moved off in another direction," Reb said, and pointed his fork at
Eloise, "Komelecki won't be needed here anyway.
German's just got a bee in his bonnet about the
man. He's always been gullible."

Eloise shook her head in warning. "Don't be so
sure it's just gullibility. Komelecki's the real thing.
Don't you read the papers? He's famous for finding
missing people and tracking down criminals."

"You know the trouble with those newspaper stories, don't you?" Reb asked. "They only report the
news. The *old* is that Komelecki probably misses
two dozen times for every hit. And when he does
find something, it's just luck."

"Excuse me." Wayne held up his hand like a
schoolboy asking permission to leave the room.
"How can you be sure the Night Terror isn't still
headed for Jesus Creek?"

We all looked at him in amazement. Hadn't he
been sitting right there listening to us? "Because,"
I told him, going slow so he could keep up, "he's
changed his pattern. Didn't you hear the broadcast
this morning? Instead of moving in a straight line,
the way he's been doing, he's headed off down south
of here."

"Could be this wasn't the same man," Wayne
pointed out. "After all, the Night Terror has estab-
lished his pattern, and the girl in Laytonville
doesn't fit. Too soon after the last time, wrong lo-
cation, sloppy handling."

"Well, Reb?" I turned to the police chief, hoping he'd share whatever information he'd received about the Laytonville situation.

"Could be the Hopkins girl was picked up by a run-of-the-mill nut," he said thoughtfully. "Or it could have been the Night Terror changing his routine." Reb poured another packet of sugar into his coffee. "I don't reckon we'll know for sure until the investigation's complete and they've decided to make a comment."

"But you're tapped into their network, aren't you?" I wasn't going to let him off that easy. "You must know something the rest of us don't."

"Who, me?" Reb shook his head with all innocence. "All I know is, people ought to take normal precautions and not get carried away with every rumor that passes through."

I refilled Wayne's coffee cup, since he'd already finished his milk. "It would be easier for us to take precautions if we knew the whole story, wouldn't it? Just tell me what you think, Reb. Was the man in Laytonville the Night Terror, or not?"

"Kay, honey, I figure the Night Terror could be sitting right here in the room with us and I wouldn't know it. I'm just a small-town cop, not Sherlock Holmes."

CHAPTER
5

The Emperor: The Journey is well under way. Now is the time to begin your adventure.

FOR THE REST OF THE DAY THE RADIO UP-dated us on developments in Laytonville. A band of law enforcement officials had descended upon that town like an Old Testament plague. I was elated. It seemed to me that, with an eyewitness to guide them, the police were bound to have the Night Terror in custody by the time my shift ended. Even if they didn't catch him right away, though, he was on the run.

Despite lack of hard evidence, we all decided to pretend the Night Terror had moved on, and Jesus Creek got back to the business of St. Patrick's Day preparations. Every customer we had for the rest of the day brought in word of folks who'd be arriving for the festivities. Frankie Mae Weathers popped in to let us know that her nephew, Walt Carhart, was planning to have the official opening of the Estelle Williams Carhart Historical Museum during the St. Pat's Day. Walt had been driving in from Nashville every weekend for months, trying to spruce up the museum (actually his late mother's house). He was bound to be glad that preparations were almost over.

Delia Cannon, who'd done almost as much work on the museum as Walt, stopped by for lunch and informed us (none too cheerfully) that her daughter and son-in-law would be staying with her for a couple of days. My favorite person, and Delia's significant other, Roger Shelton, came in with her and was immediately surrounded by the other customers, all of whom wanted information about the new statue.

"I hear the statue's in place," I said, setting Roger's coffee on the table. "With armed guards, no less." How Roger persuaded people to stand outside all night with baseball bats for weapons, I couldn't imagine—but he probably promised them something illegal for their efforts.

"I made a solemn vow," Roger told me, raising his right hand, "to my fellow members of the Historical Society. And I will die, if I must, to protect my honor." Then, dropping his hand, he added, "But, damn, I didn't know people would take this so seriously. My phone is ringing all day and night, little old ladies accost me on the street. . . . I never realized that popularity came with power."

What Roger seemed to have missed was that those old ladies had been after him all along. He's tall and lean and generally decked out in jeans, but on the rare occasions when I've seen him in a suit and tie—oh, my goodness! Even I could succumb to his craggy smile and blue eyes.

So for whatever reason, Roger had become a popular man in Jesus Creek, except within the confines of the SDC. Since he isn't eligible to join their organization (descendants of Confederate soldiers only), he'd taken his membership to the Historical Society. The latter group consists mostly of old ladies with too much time and money who skitter about town raising funds for silly projects, or scout the local churches for single men in the proper age group. They practically begged for Roger's membership. It didn't seem to matter that he was already sinfully smitten with Delia—he was a man and he showed up for meetings.

Three of the biddies were circling around him as he and Delia tried to eat lunch. Delia didn't appear to mind all the attention he gathered, nor the fact that he was wallowing in it. When I could finally push my way through the crowd to refill Roger's coffee cup, I couldn't help but ask, "Delia, has it occurred to you that this man could be the Night Terror?"

"I've known for quite some time that he is a night terror," she told me sweetly. "But at his age, it's to be expected. Snores, you know."

"I don't snore," Roger said confidently, as if he had proof. "Delia's just ticked off because I won't tell her who's under the sheet."

"I don't care," Delia said, and her lack of interest sounded genuine to me. "But I strongly suspect, from the way you've been grinning to yourself lately, that the town at large may not approve."

"How can they not? The town chose the subject."

Delia gave him her schoolteacher look, the one that meant she knew perfectly well he'd been smoking in the bathroom and he needn't bother to deny it. "Don't expect me to defend you," she told him.

"Maybe if you tell me about the statue, I could offer refuge," I said. "Also I could get rich making bets."

Roger pressed one finger firmly to his lips and mumbled, "Mmphgrb Mlptygrb."

"Oh, goodie! That's who I voted for." I poured his coffee and winked at Delia. She was probably right. Roger wasn't above stuffing the ballot box. And if he was that happy about the statue, it had to be the likeness of someone the Sons and Daughters of the Confederacy wouldn't admit to the human race.

Just then, as if on cue, Sarah Elizabeth Leach, the SDC's new secretary, waddled through the door and dashed over to join Delia and Roger. It took her a few seconds to tuck her stomach under the table, but all in all, she moved pretty well for a woman on the brink of the blessed event. "Don't tell anyone I was here," she said breathlessly.

"Okay," Delia agreed. "How about lunch?"

"Yes." Sarah Elizabeth looked up at me and with pleading eyes said, "Anything, with mashed potatoes and gravy, cornbread with extra butter, and some kind of gooey pie for dessert. Try to find a piece with extra meringue."

I nodded and jotted down the order on my notepad. "Mother-in-law been after you again?" I asked.

Sarah Elizabeth sighed. "For dinner last night I had salad. For breakfast, low-cal yogurt and fruit. I've had my doctor talk to her, and he's explained repeatedly that pregnant women are allowed to gain weight. But Mother Eliza is convinced that I'm making the child fat. Do you know, she even runs raids on the library? Just to be sure I'm not hiding food there. Which I am, of course."

"Don't worry, I'll never tell a soul. I'm not sure how we'll get Roger to swear secrecy, though."

Roger shook his head. "Don't be silly, Kay. I've never been able to stand Eliza. Anything that aggravates her ulcer is perfectly all right with me." He smiled encouragingly at Sarah Elizabeth.

I left Delia and Roger sheltering Sarah Elizabeth. Benny and Chester had taken up residence at their favorite table. The coffee drinkers had begun to arrive for a second round. Back in the kitchen, Eloise and the cook were giggling over a dirty joke they'd shared, and out front the coffeepot was briskly brewing. It's moments of harmony and contentment like these that make my life complete.

By the end of the day I'd almost forgotten about the Night Terror. The afternoon conversation at Eloise's had centered around the unveiling of the statue, the possibility of rain on the seventeenth, and Glenda Richmond's chances of winning the Miss North America pageant. (These contests never end. If she won Miss North America, Glenda would then vie for the title of Miss United World.)

I walked home, enjoying the February dusk and the sight of hills backlighted by the setting sun. In summer, when the hills are solid green, I understand why people never seem to want to leave this town. Even in winter, the atmosphere around Jesus Creek can be comforting, as if someone's wrapped a gigantic blanket around us all, and the hills are a mother's arms tucking us in.

Bella met me at the door, hissed, then padded over to John and curled up in his lap. After shucking my coat and purse, I picked up the mail John had piled on the coffee table. A water bill and a rejection slip. How could I tell, you may ask, that it was a rejection slip? Because any envelope that's addressed to me and still shows folding creases is clearly a self-addressed stamped envelope. And this particular one was too fat to contain only a cheery note from a friendly editor who'd loved my poems.

An eternal optimist, I opened it anyway, only to

discover that *these came close.* I threw the envelope, poems, and cryptic rejection on the table.

John was sprawled across the couch, absently stroking Bella and reading the Nashville newspaper. He's a news junkie and has the ability to remember every detail of every report no matter how dreary. Tonight he seemed positively entranced.

"I don't suppose they've caught him?" I asked hopefully.

John shook his head. "Nowhere near. I'd say the authorities are completely baffled." He held up the front page. "Look at this. Communiqué from the killer."

"Are you serious?" I snatched the paper from his hand and sure enough, there it was—a letter from the Night Terror. It was addressed to the editor in chief, according to the caption, and had been reproduced in its entirety:

> You have worked so hard and expended so much time trying to understand my work. I feel sorry for you and also I like the game we can play this way so I am writing to help you. Some of you are hunters just like me. Animals are animals and sport is sport. But I like to be artistic as you have no doubt noticed.

I looked up at John. "What does he mean, he likes to be artistic? Is he painting murals at the crime scenes or something?"

"Probably information about the case that the public doesn't have yet," John suggested.

"I heard they're holding back on some things— clues left at the scenes, I guess."

"They are. But the bottom line is that they don't know what's going on. The Night Terror has them stumped. Read the rest of it."

I went back to the paper. The letter had been handwritten, and the penmanship was atrocious, I might add. It was difficult to decipher some of the words.

Some killers are legendary but some are great. The great ones of course have never been captured. It remains to be seen if I will fall into that category but if your investigations continue as they have I expect to achieve the honor with ease. Perhaps you would have an easier time if you told the people more about my work. All eyes would then be on the alert. Or perhaps more knowledge of me would just terrify. Are you afraid of creating panic? Believe me panic would ensue if any of you knew my plans. But do not give up yet. I will be with you for a long long time. There is still a chance that you will come to understand me. I doubt if you will stop me.

"He's an arrogant SOB, isn't he?" I handed the paper back to John. "But he's made a serious mistake now. Surely they can get some clues from this letter. And the girl in Laytonville can probably give them a full description."

"He wouldn't have written the letter if he thought it would help the police," John pointed out. "That's part of the fun of it for him. He's getting right in their faces and they're stumped."

"For now, maybe. But sooner or later they'll catch him. I just hope it's sooner—before he decides to visit Jesus Creek, after all." I hung my jacket in the front closet, kicked off the sensible shoes I wear for work, and joined John on the sofa. "Isn't there anything on TV? A mindless sitcom, maybe, or a game show?"

"Reality programming, you mean?" John winked at me. He always winks when he thinks he's confused me.

"You consider reality a game show, is that it? I'll bite. What's my prize if I guess the answers?"

John eased Bella onto the floor. Then he sat up and pulled the tarot pack from his shirt pocket. "Fulfillment. Let's see what your cards say today."

He handed me the deck, and I shuffled three times, then cut before handing them back. I watched as John spread them carefully on the coffee table in the shape of a cross. "You're suffering a great deal of conflict right now, aren't you?" he said.

Well, heck, I thought, isn't everyone?

"It goes directly back to this card—" He pointed, but I didn't pay much attention, since I'd long ago decided that John improvises as he goes along. "—the one that signifies your mother. Have you called her lately?"

"No," I said. "You know I never call Mother unless I need money more than peace of mind."

"Perhaps you'd like to work on that at the next twelve-step meeting. You know, you'll never be healthy until you've resolved your conflicting feelings about your mother."

"My feelings do not conflict. I like her just fine as long as I'm here and she's in Florida. What else can the cards tell me?"

"Now this might interest you." He pointed to the King of Cups. "Any new men in your life?"

I started to tell him that the only men in my life weren't new; instead they were getting old real quick. I reconsidered—first of all, because John had told me repeatedly that one shouldn't inject a flip attitude into a tarot reading, and second, because sometimes he gets his feelings hurt over the silliest comments. "No," I said. "No new men."

"One's on the way, then. This is your future. And this card relates directly to the king—you're going to have to make a choice concerning this man. But choose carefully."

"What sort of choice? Whether to serve him coffee or tea? Whether to get in the car with him and ride out to a deserted, wooded area late at night?" Sometimes I can't help myself. John's readings are like those daily horoscopes in the newspaper. Just vague enough to apply to anybody.

"There's a good chance you'll make the right choice," he went on, "because here's the High Priestess. That represents you, Kay. A woman of wisdom, well on her way to emotional balance."

"Last time you pulled that card for yourself, you said the High Priestess was the perfect woman."

John gathered up the cards, then shuffled them absently a few times. "The meaning depends on the position of the card, its place in relation to the others. It's also a personal interpretation. The cards mean different things to different readers. I've developed a relationship with my tarot pack."

"And I'm ecstatic for you, John," I told him. "Is there anything to eat? Or do we have to cook?"

John rose and stretched his arms above his head. "There's hamburger. We'd better consider going to the store soon."

I nodded and stood up myself. "I'll stop by the grocery on my way home tomorrow. Anything special you want?"

"Coffee," he said, predictably. "French roast would be nice."

That was a joke. You see, grocery shopping in Jesus Creek is like grocery shopping in the Soviet Union. You can't go down the aisle picking up the items on your list. Instead you buy what's available and try to make the best of it.

I'd followed John into the kitchen, where we both poked our heads into the refrigerator. I knew sandwiches were out because I'd already seen the empty bread wrapper folded neatly on the countertop. John insists on hoarding them because, he says, it's one little step toward saving the planet—and because they *look* so useful. (I'd once purchased a set of Ginsu knives for that very reason: they looked useful. So far I've never chopped through a steak bone *or* a tin can.)

"I'm pretty sure I can find coffee. But if not, will chocolate serve the purpose?"

"Dark chocolate," he said. He pulled out the hamburger and held it in his hand for a minute, weighing the possibilities. "Hamburgers?"

"Chili," I suggested.

"Spaghetti?"

"Let's feed it to Bella and go to Benton Harbor for catfish."

John pitched the meat back into the fridge and slammed the door. "I'll treat. You know, one of us ought to learn to cook."

"Or one of us ought to *marry* a cook. Doesn't that seem easier?"

"Given the losers we've attached ourselves to in the past, I'd say not." John picked up his wallet from the kitchen counter and headed out the back door without waiting for me. He knew I'd follow. I'm codependent.

CHAPTER

6

The Hierophant: You seek the approval of all those you
meet along the way.

RIDING IN A CAR WITH JOHN SULLIVAN IS A
unique experience. He drives as if the license ev-
aluator is looking over his shoulder. He stops at
yield signs, gives a turn signal for miles before he
actually makes the move, and slows for a yellow
light instead of trying to run it. Frankly, he makes
me crazy. But he also has some sort of macho hang-
up that won't allow him to ride in a car being driven
by a woman, so we made our way slowly, steadily,
and safely to Benton Harbor.

Benton Harbor is west of Jesus Creek, just
across the Tennessee River. As if drawn by an un-
inspired artist, the landscape changes at the
county line from comfortable rolling hills to stark
flatlands.

The sun had all but dropped below the horizon
when we crossed the river. A few hardy fishermen
were reeling in their boats at the dock, and one

sailboat was drifting into the distance. The river scares heck out of me, but I love to drive over it. Trees hadn't yet leafed out, so the oaks and maples along the shore were tall and black, stark against the sun reflected in the water.

"River's calm tonight," John said, and actually took his eyes off the road for a second to admire the view.

"This is the kind of evening that heals raw souls," I agreed. "Maybe you should bring that kid out here. What's his name? Todd?"

"Scott," John corrected. "Scott Carter. He's already been here—one night after his father gave him a bloody nose. Told me he stood on the bridge and almost jumped."

"That's frightening. How old is the boy?"

"Too damn young to die." John was silent for a few minutes.

I'd learned that that sort of fierce comment followed by silence was an indication that John was furious and trying to get a hold on his emotions. He doesn't like to let go, doesn't want anyone to think he might be out of control. I figured it had to do with all those years of alcohol, when, according to John, he was often so unhinged that he didn't even remember where he was.

"Do you think he's getting better?" I asked finally.

"Scott? Maybe. I've never met anyone with so much hostility. I've worked with kids who had more right to anger, if you can believe that, but Scott doesn't seem to have any sort of constructive outlet. Everything is turned inward. He lets it sit inside until he can't take the pressure anymore, then he explodes. And does something stupid, like climbing on a bridge and throwing one leg over."

"But he didn't jump," I pointed out. "Doesn't that

mean he's got a desire to live? At least a little hope?"

"Or it could mean that he *had* hope. He was younger then, less bitter. Next time ... I don't know what he might do if he starts feeling that pressure again. Scott has to make a choice—whether to blame fate for his miserable existence and continue along the path he's treading now, or take responsibility for his own state of mind."

"Which do you think he'll do?" I know human behavior is unpredictable, but John is almost as good as that psychic Komelecki when it comes to predicting behavior.

"I've offered him a hand," he said. "Something to grab hold of. If he accepts the offer, I can lead him to himself. He has talent, you know. You saw that old bike he's driving. Scott keeps it running. The only class he hasn't been thrown out of is auto shop. The boy's a near genius when it comes to mechanical repairs. But ultimately it's his choice, isn't it?"

"Couldn't he be mired in one of those stages teenagers suffer through? Maybe he's just feeling neglected and wants someone to pay attention to him."

"Of course he feels neglected. He hasn't found the strength to turn up his nose at other people and their opinions of him. Oh, he *claims* he doesn't care. But he's desperate for attention and he's willing to do almost anything to get it. Some kids get parental love in return for good grades, or sports achievements. Scott's parents aren't going to love him no matter what he does. That goes down hard. He can't admit it. So he tries to force them to feel *something*."

"Like what? Regret that they didn't treat him

better when he was alive? A lot of good that'll do Scott from his grave."

"That's just what he's aiming for."

I felt my codependent nature kick in. "Let's invite him over one night. I'll order pizza."

"There's nothing a kid hates more than some softhearted adult pretending to be friendly."

We'd just reached the Benton Harbor city limits and the river was behind us. I wished John would turn on the radio, to break the silence. I hadn't liked Scott when I first met him. I wasn't sure I ever would like the child. But I felt that old familiar tug on my heart and regretted having made the crack about drowning him. If John couldn't straighten him out, no one could. And I knew John could do anything he set his mind to.

Staying sober for ten years toughens you up.

Catfish Heaven was almost empty, which pleased me immensely. John seemed a bit disappointed, though. One of his favorite games is Long-Distance Analysis. He watches other diners—their body movements, facial expressions, and so forth—then tells me their problems. A typical meal goes something like this: "See how she's leaning away from him, ordering without consulting him at all. Look, now she's trying to talk him out of getting what he really wants. He's going along with her, just to keep peace. But look at his face. He's managed to wipe her right out of his reality. See how she's sitting now. Very straight and pleased with herself because she thinks she's had the last word. But look at him. I'll bet he'd like a little leather once in a while."

You can understand why I chose an isolated corner table, away from the few other customers.

While the waitress scurried around us, I introduced John to my own problem. "You haven't run into our newest resident, have you? Wayne Holland?"

John drained his coffee cup and began to fidget right away. I've told him repeatedly to order it by the pot. "No," he said, flapping his arms wildly to get the waitress's attention. "At least, I haven't noticed any new dings in the car." Rim shot.

"He's just moved here," I went on. "Been coming to the diner. Long hair. Earring."

"Your dream man. Remember the cards."

I remembered, but the King of Cups had absolutely nothing to do with this. "Not likely. In fact, it's crossed my mind that he might be our serial killer. You know that girl in Laytonville? Well, Wayne was telling us that she probably was not attacked by the Night Terror. He said it didn't fit the pattern. And the abduction was haphazard."

"He's right. These attacks have consistently occurred every ten days. The bodies have been found fifty miles apart, in a direct line from east to west. And the victims were blondes." Having attracted a waitress, John requested an immediate refill of his cup, along with an individual pot. When the waitress had satisfied his caffeine craving, he went on. "The Laytonville girl—what's her name? Cathy?— was in the wrong place, on the wrong date, and wearing the wrong hair."

"What do you mean?"

"I saw her sobbing out her story on the news. She's a brunette, and none too attractive. Obviously starved for attention. Probably wishes the Night Terror *would* get her."

"John!" I exploded. "That's a crude and sexist remark." Given my earlier comment about young Scott Carter, I suddenly realized that we were one

for one with insensitive observations. Naturally, I
did not mention this aloud. Instead there was a
brief silence, during which I refilled my own cup
from the pot. "So she was not a victim of the Night
Terror?"

"Probably not," John agreed. "But he could have
changed his modus operandi."

"Why?"

John leaned back in his chair and slipped into
the monotone he adopts when he lectures. Must be
hard for his students to stay awake when he does
that in class. "Self-esteem killers want to make an
impression on the world. Which is why they don't
kill quietly and get away with it. Except for the
highly intelligent ones, like Jack the Ripper, of
course, but old Jack falls into the sex-killer category. Anyway, the point is to establish a pattern
that can be traced, so as to focus attention upon the
killer's power."

"Then he'd want to stick to the pattern, wouldn't
he? To *keep* attention focused on himself?"

"Yes, unless he's starting a new pattern."

"Pattern," I said, excited by a thought that had
just dropped into my head. "If we got a map and
marked the sites where bodies have been found,
there might be a pattern! The killer could be creating a circle or a star, for instance." I stopped to
think. "But why would he do that?"

"Maybe he gets his kicks by driving cops crazy."

"Wonderful," I said, wishing I'd worn a hat over
my own brunette hair, just in case. "But never
mind. I only brought this up because of Wayne Holland. There's something about the man that jars
me. I really think he might be dangerous."

"He's getting through your defenses, Kay.
That's why he jars. Don't you think it's time you
stopped closing yourself off to men? At least give

Mr. Holland a chance to know you." And then, in a singsong voice, he added, "Ka-ay's got a boyfriend."

"Nonsense. I'd be the first to notice. I want your serious opinion. The man seems so . . . nice."

"Yeah, that's an unmistakable mark of the serial killer. Underneath that wholesome exterior beats the heart of a real sick puppy. Of course, that's just what would attract you."

That was encouraging. And John was right: I did fall for men who would win the Neurotic of the Year Award. But I'd known that for a long time, even if I hadn't actualized it. I still felt that I could, with some careful exploration of my personality, have an intimate and fulfilling relationship with a healthy man. It was the other part that worried me. What if I really did find Wayne . . . well, interesting? There was absolutely nothing to indicate that he was not a normal human being. Except for my quite minimal interest in him. And perhaps my mental health had improved so much that I could— No, I decided; I wasn't sufficiently recovered to trust my instincts.

Our catfish dinners threatened to spill off the oversize plates before the waitress got them from tray to table. Then she had to return to the kitchen for John's next pot of coffee. I made a mental note to leave her a large tip (since John never remembers to tip at all) and dug into my extra order of hush puppies.

"You don't think Wayne's the killer then?" I asked.

"Could I meet him before I give you an answer?" John asked sweetly. "I'm good, but even I have to meet the subject to form an opinion of his problems."

I could have pointed out that he'd often made a

diagnosis without fulfilling this requirement, but I believe that meals should be made as stress-free as possible. "You'll run into him at Eloise's sooner or later. He's moved into Roger's old apartment and he doesn't seem to like cooking any more than we do."

"I ran into Roger this morning, by the way. He tried to get me to sign up for statue duty. I noticed the statue was being guarded by Benny and Chester this afternoon, so I suppose Roger takes just anybody who happens along," John said. "They've taken to the job. Gives them a chance to pretend at power."

"What's Roger Shelton up to?" I asked. "Why has he gotten involved in this silly project?"

"Maybe he's endearing himself to the citizenry so they won't suspect that he's really the Night Terror."

Well, I knew that was ridiculous. I didn't even consider the possibility that good old Rog had been on a killing spree. Not for more than a second, anyway. "I'm asking for your professional opinion. Why has Roger suddenly taken interest in community affairs?"

"Roger? He likes to manipulate other people. Don't be surprised when the statue turns out to be no one anybody voted for. But since Roger carefully placed himself in the position of ballot counter, and since none of the old ladies thought to check up on him, no one will ever know."

"Oh, I think we'll know. If you're right, then Roger will have chosen the subject for the statue himself. That shouldn't be hard to miss. The only thing is, if Roger did that, someone may string him up right in front of his precious statue."

"What a clever idea. I wonder if the Night Terror

has thought of leaving a body in our own little park?" John started ripping his catfish apart, while I tried not to choke on my coleslaw.

CHAPTER

7

The Lovers: Temptation beckons.

"I'VE BEEN UP ALL NIGHT," WAYNE HOL-
land said wearily, and signaled for a cup of coffee
by pointing to the pot.

"Still trying to get unpacked?" I set a steaming
cup of fresh brew in front of him, along with sugar
and cream. He ignored the latter. I felt a twinge of
sympathy for the man when I remembered my own
moving experiences. Those boxes seemed to breed
while I slept, so that no matter how much junk I
disposed of or stored, there was always more. And
truly useful items disappeared into that black hole
that also claims socks and cigarette lighters. To this
day I haven't found my Tupperware Jell-O mold.

"I finished that about two A.M.," he said, and
yawned. "But I have to get ready for graveyards
tonight. Sort of like working an extra one. So to
keep myself awake I took my dirty clothes over to
the Wash-o-Rama and did laundry half the night."

The cook slapped the little bell in the serving

window to let me know he had breakfast ready for
Benny and Chester, but Eloise grabbed the plates
before I could get to them. "You go ahead and take
Wayne's order." She gave me a sly wink and took
off.

Reluctantly I turned to Wayne. "Are you in the
mood for eggs?" I asked him. "Or a cheeseburger?"

Wayne shook his head. "Just the coffee. Give me
some time to think about the other. I've been stuffing myself with Oreos all night."

"Sure. No hurry." I hoped that when he finally
decided to eat, I'd be major busy with something
else. It bothered me that the man was so damned
polite. I couldn't legally dislike him unless he gave
me a reason. And I desperately wanted to dislike
him. While he sat there looking exhausted and di-
sheveled, and while I pondered the sad plight of a
man doing his own laundry in the middle of the
night, I'd begun to feel a bit, well, attracted to him.
Actually, I reminded myself, what I felt was sympathy and the codependent's need to make everything better for him. This is not a good basis for a
relationship. And it's exactly how I'd gotten myself
into unprofitable relationships in the past.

Our coffee drinkers started to wander in and
gather at the center table. It's an interesting assortment—some in suits and ties, others in overalls
and work shirts. I don't think their dress has anything to do with money, though, because they seem
to take turns buying coffee for each other. Some of
them just prefer to dress better than others.

"Go ahead and bring another cup," Will Davis
told me. "I saw Frank Pate headed this way when
I came in."

So I loaded up a tray with cups and carried the
pot in my other hand. "You fellas ready for the parade?" I asked.

Almost all of them were involved in the St. Pat celebration. The store owners would decorate their businesses, and several would sponsor parade entries. Anyone with a tractor would be using it to pull floats. Several of our coffee drinkers are on the volunteer fire department, and they spend a good week shining up the engine, which leads the parade every year.

"Shoot, yeah," Will said. "I got a box in the back of the store marked *parade*. I just haul it out every year and tell the girls in the front to fix things up."

Will is our town chauvinist. The *girls* who work for him have been eligible for retirement for about a decade now. But I guess if they don't mind his attitude, I shouldn't worry on their behalf.

"Sure glad that serial killer decided to head off in another direction." Paul Hobel held up his cup. "We got enough to do around here without having a bunch of cops swarming all over the place. Hey, Kay. Reckon this cup's got a hole in the bottom?"

Don't ever say that to a waitress. It is not an original line. I gritted my teeth and refilled his cup anyway.

"Heard about Jackson's barn burnin' last night?" Will Davis asked. "Seems to me they ought to be able to catch whoever did it easy enough, after all them fires we had last fall."

"Yeah? What makes you think that?"

Before Will could get rolling, I took my pot and empty tray back behind the counter. The second coffee maker was just finishing up, so I turned the setting to warm and started the first one again.

"I guess I'll try breakfast," Wayne said finally.

Where the hell was Eloise? She'd disappeared while I was at the coffee drinkers' table, so there was no choice but to wait on Wayne. I'd just have to be mature about this, I realized. Simply because

I felt sorry for the man didn't mean I had to feel anything else for him. That, I suspected, was the sign of a truly healthy individual. Perhaps I was getting better.

"Fried eggs?" I asked, remembering what he'd ordered every day so far. "Sausage? Biscuits and gravy?"

"Pretty good," he said with surprise. "How do you do that?"

"Practice," I told him, and wrote the order out for the cook. "I see you're still wearing the same earring. How many do you have?"

Wayne reached up and fingered the cross dangling from his left ear. "I've got a bunch, but most of them are the same. You know, I have to buy two just alike because I can't find anyplace that'll break up a pair."

He sounded so seriously offended, I couldn't help laughing. "Tell you what," I offered, "I'm always losing half a pair. Why don't I give you my leftovers?"

That made him laugh. "Good deal. Or if you have a yard sale, I'll just stop in and buy a few. I'd hate to take your earrings for nothing."

Yard sale. I made a mental note to hold one as soon as the weather became more dependable. No telling how much money I could get for that old shower curtain. "If I have a sale, I'll let you know. You can have first pick. I hope you don't mind cheap jewelry."

"With what's left of my salary, I can't afford to be choosy."

I wondered briefly what part of his salary went to the ex-wife. It didn't seem quite fair that he'd have to pay alimony, since she was employed herself. There I go again, I thought, remembering that I had no idea what the former Mrs. Holland might have suffered through. Although honestly I couldn't imagine Wayne being all *that* difficult to live with.

"I'd better take this off while I'm thinking about it." He reached up and pulled the earring out of his lobe. "I'm having dinner with my folks tonight and they can't handle it."

"And where do your folks live?" I asked, but only for the sake of conversation.

"Benton Harbor," he said, tucking the earring into his shirt pocket. "I used to spend more time with 'em, but between moving and shift work it hasn't been easy. Ah, hell. That's not a very good excuse for neglecting my family, is it?"

I felt my resolve turning to mush. Here was this sensitive man, worrying about neglecting his aged parents, and I'd thought he might be a serial killer. I almost invited him to dinner right there, but a vision of John's smirk stopped me.

"It's real nice of you to worry about your folks." I turned away from him to run a cloth across the metal of the coffeepot. I counted to ten and found that the urge to mother Wayne Holland was almost gone.

Suddenly the door slammed open, and Roger Shelton strode in. He waved broadly to everyone in the place, slapped a few of the men on their surprised backs, and took a stool next to Wayne.

"Good morning, Kay!" he boomed. "Morning, Frank. How you boys doin' on this fine day?" He settled himself at the counter and continued to exude unnatural cheerfulness as he smiled and nodded at the other diners.

"You've got to stop this," I warned him. "We've gotten used to your insults and sneaky ways. How can we trust you if you keep on being friendly?"

Roger motioned for me to come closer, then whispered, "It's all part of a grand plan."

"Really?" Okay. I was willing to play along with him. I'm one of the few people in town who can abide Roger. It's been suggested, in fact, that he and I were Siamese twins in a previous life. Which wouldn't surprise me. The only difference between Roger and me is that he has the guts to *say* what I only *think*.

I set a cup of coffee down in front of him (the last drops from the pot—just the way Roger likes it) and waited for his explanation.

"You see," he said after a hit of caffeine, "I hope to replace Constance Winter."

Constance Winter had been our resident loony for years. Since her recent illness and incarceration in the Jesus Creek Nursing Home, the town had been thuddingly dull.

"I think you've got a darned good shot at it, Roger," I said supportively.

"Wonderful! If I try hard, I expect that one day the good people of Jesus Creek will refer to me as *that crazy old coot*."

"What makes you think they don't already?" Eloise asked, appearing from nowhere.

"If they did," Roger countered, "I'd get more respect. For a while it bothered me—you know, that lunatics were revered, while exceptionally intelligent men like myself were demeaned and maligned. But I think I've figured it out. The world appreciates a unique individual."

I thought if that were true, everyone in town would be worshiped, but I didn't tell Roger. It's not a good idea to give him fodder.

Turning to Wayne he said, "Like this gentleman. Don't believe I caught your name, sir."

This was going to be fun. I'd wondered why Roger was ignoring someone of Wayne's obviously unique nature. Now I saw that Wayne was about to become the next victim of Roger's sardonic wit.

Wayne executed a snap-to that would have done any recruit proud. "Wayne Holland," he said, extending his hand.

"Roger Shelton, aspiring psychotic. I couldn't help noticing that you're a good-size man. Work out, do you?"

"Not if I can help it," Wayne said uncertainly.

"The reason I ask"—and here Roger leaned in to his conspirator pose again—"is that I need a few reliable men. To guard a statue."

"A statue?" Poor old Wayne was new to town, so he hadn't heard about the park statue yet. "Is someone trying to steal it?"

"No, no. But someone will probably try to look at it."

"You don't want anyone to look at the statue?" To his credit, Wayne hadn't leapt from his seat and sought shelter yet. But he appeared a mite anxious.

"Not until it's officially unveiled," Roger explained. "I have a couple of local farmers with pitchforks, but a fella your size could probably do the job of two of them. What do you say? Could you hold down the fort a couple of days?"

"Are we talking about twenty-four-hour shifts or what?"

I was truly amazed that Wayne was taking the request seriously. So was everyone else in the place. They'd all stopped talking to eavesdrop on the conversation.

"Heavens, no. A man can't operate at peak efficiency without rest." Roger whipped out his wallet and pulled from it a piece of paper, which he carefully unfolded and spread on the counter in front of him. "Now here's the schedule. You can see the hours that are unclaimed. Just pick your time."

Wayne looked the list over carefully, then pulled
a pencil from his shirt pocket and wrote his name
on three of the open squares. "Are you providing
the weapons? Or should I bring my own bazooka?"

Eloise laughed first. It took the rest of us a few
seconds to realize that Roger had failed pitifully in
his attempt to put one over on the newcomer.

Just after the lunch crowd left we saw Reb's pa-
trol car scream past the diner, lights flashing and
siren blaring. About two minutes later the town's
only ambulance whizzed by, also in full emergency
mode. Eloise and I stood beside the two straggling
customers and pressed our noses to the window. Apparently the excitement was located somewhere on
the east side of town.

Of course, it could have been an accident. In fact,
someone suggested that at the time. But I know *I*
felt a tingle down my spine that assured me it was
something far, far worse than minor injuries. Call
it woman's intuition or just morbid imagination—I
knew that the killer had struck again.

Eloise and I busied ourselves for the next half
hour with menial chores. Every few minutes one of
us would wander over to the front door and gaze
eastward. "I oughta get a police scanner in here,"
Eloise said at one point. "I just hate suspense."

"We could call the police department and ask the
dispatcher what's going on," I suggested.

"They wouldn't tell us anything. I've tried it."
Eloise looked wistfully at the phone, though.

When Henry Mooten came in, his face was whiter
than chalk and his hands shook, so I thought we
might finally be having that earthquake. "Give me
some coffee, Eloise," he said without preamble.

Eloise poured out a cup and asked sharply,
"What's happened, Henry?"

He slugged down about half the coffee before he answered. "They started tearing down the Host place this morning."

The Host house had burned several months before, and the owners were only now getting around to the business of demolishing the shell. I didn't think for a minute that the loss of a local landmark was what had Henry upset.

"You know how them bushes used to grow right across the back of the lot there." Henry used his hand to describe the evenly trimmed shrubs that marked the Host boundary. "One of the workers was out that way and he found something."

Eloise and I waited quietly, if not patiently. Henry seemed to be having enough trouble getting out the story. He didn't need us nagging him for details.

"He found a body," Henry said at last. "It's a girl. Well, woman I guess you'd have to say. Reb's out there now and I reckon he's already figured out who she is. I left when they got to talking about specifics. Some things a regular person don't need to know." He emptied his coffee cup and held it out for a refill.

There didn't seem to be any way to ask the questions piling up in my head, so I poured coffee for Henry, then filled up two more cups for Eloise and me. So, I thought, the Night Terror found us. He's been here. He's resumed the pattern, just as the experts had predicted.

"I don't know," Henry mumbled, surely talking to himself and not to us, "but it seems like there's been some sort of curse dumped on this town. Maybe that quake's the only thing that's gonna put a stop to it."

CHAPTER
8

The Chariot, reversed: Beware the impulse that urges you on to recklessness.

JOHN CAME IN JUST AFTER HENRY LEFT. BY that time Eloise and I had finished cleaning up the after-lunch chaos and were slumped on counter stools, exhausted from work and the news of a new victim.

"You look like a couple of hens on a roost pole," John told us.

"Mind your manners, boy, or I'll give the leftovers to some other stray." Eloise threw one arm around John and gave him a motherly hug.

Recognizing a warm welcome, John joined us at the counter. "Reading?" he asked Eloise, indicating his tarot pack.

"Some other time, darlin'. Right now I don't want to know about the future."

"They found a body in the Host yard," I explained. "We just heard about it from Henry Mooten."

John's expression was grim. "Someone from Jesus Creek?"

"Henry didn't know. I expect Reb will be in for his supper after while and I'll find out then." Eloise scooted off her stool and went into the kitchen to fix a plate for John. She feeds him often, always refusing to let him pay. She claims it's because he's practically a relative of an employee. Truth is, she's a soft touch and knows he's always broke.

"Henry didn't know any more than that?" John asked me.

"Nope. And I'm sure as hell not going down there to find out for myself." I felt inexplicably calm. Perhaps I was in a state of denial. Then again, maybe I was just selfishly pleased that it wasn't *my* body they were hauling off in a bag.

I finished the soft drink I'd been sipping on and started to toss the can in the trash, but John stopped me. "That's recyclable, you know."

I set the can on the counter to quiet him. "I've been thinking about this killer. You know, they profile these guys. I don't know how, but Clara Maddox mentioned it. Seems to me there ought to be enough information floating around by now to catch him."

"Not if he's clever enough," John pointed out. "Lots of killers never get caught. Most of them, probably."

"Well, by God, this one will." I was suddenly furious. How dare some homicidal maniac invade my town? And in the spirit of do-gooders everywhere, I was determined to throw myself fully into the manhunt. "There must be a pattern. Let's start with that."

While I mused, John ignored me. I got the distinct impression that he thought I was being silly, but I didn't much care. Someone had to track down the Night Terror, and I figured the more of us who worked on the project, the faster we'd get him. I saw no reason why I couldn't put clues together as well as anyone else.

"I suppose," John said after a brief silence, "that you're waiting for me to comment."

I hadn't been waiting for that at all. "Sure, John," I agreed. "Why don't you shuffle the cards and see if you can pick up on the killer?"

"You have such a one-track mind. There are professionals to track criminals. Let them do their jobs without interference."

"Did I say I would interfere? I'll just go along minding my own business, and if I discover anything that might be useful, I'll mention it to Reb. No big deal."

"For the sake of argument, how are you going to go about investigating this? Show up on national television and challenge the Night Terror to a face-to-face debate?"

"I'll tell you what I'm going to do." I leaned forward and looked him right in the eye. "I'm going to spread the word. Women all over this state are going to mobilize. We're going to arm ourselves and be ready for the Night Terror. And when next he meets up with one of us, he's going to have a fight on his hands." I finished with a triumphant fist in the air.

"I'd like to hear about the emotional trauma that created this need to protect the world. What sort of dangers are you protecting us from?"

"Just any that come along." I tried to sound neutral. If I sounded defensive, I knew John would spend the rest of the night psychoanalyzing my formative years.

"Here ya go, hon." Eloise returned and served John a plate loaded down with meat and gravy and

mashed potatoes. She knew better than to offer him
anything fresh and green. John believes that hu-
mans were kicked out of the Garden of Eden for
eating fruit, you see. From that he's concluded that
man was meant to live on grease, salt, chocolate,
and, of course, caffeine.

"I heard you all the way in the kitchen, Kay,"
Eloise said to me. "And I don't blame you for being
mad. Hell, so am I. But you stay out of Reb's way,
you hear? Don't you know what happens to little
girls who stir up the big, bad wolf?"

"Frankly, Eloise, I don't care. Look, if I don't stiff
my drug supplier, I probably won't be shot down in
the street. If I take an iron skillet to the first man
who tries to punch me out, I probably won't be another victim of domestic violence. But do you realize that ordinary women who've never done anyone
harm are the most likely to be killed by this Night
Terror?"

"Not if they use common sense and—"

"And what? Behave themselves? Stay locked up
at home? Well, I'll be damned if he's going to turn
me into a quivering prisoner! You know, the trouble with us is we've all been taught to be ladies.
I'll bet the reason none of the Night Terror's victims got away is because every one of them had
been told not to make a scene."

"Kay." John tapped my shoulder. "You're over-
wrought."

"I have every right to be. Women have suffered
at the hands of men long enough! It's time we threw
off the chains of—"

"So, how's the job?" Eloise jumped in. She always takes John's side.

"Scott Carter had another confrontation at school
today."

"Really?" I was only half listening, still caught up in my own battles. "What happened?"

"Isn't he that skinny boy with the motorbike?" Eloise asked. Naturally she'd know him. "His momma sure has her hands full. What's Scott into now?"

"Fistfight this time. Scott threw the first punch, of course. Apparently the other boy made a comment Scott didn't like."

"What sort of comment?"

"Who knows? It wouldn't necessarily have to be anything significant. But it shows that Scott may be sliding backward. He hasn't done anything like that for a few weeks now. I'd hoped we were getting somewhere."

"What happened after the fight? Did you talk to Scott?" I asked.

John shook his head. "He was suspended immediately. I didn't hear about it until he'd already left."

"Is it possible that Scott didn't start the fight? Maybe—"

"It's possible. But that behavior is in line with his previous acts of aggression. And the fact that he didn't ask to talk to me suggests that he was guilty and he knew it."

"When will he be back in school then?"

"The suspension lasts three days. I don't know if he'll be back after that or not. At this point he probably perceives school as an arena. The simplest thing for him to do is stay away, blaming all his troubles on the system."

"I honestly don't know how you expect to get through to this boy. He's made up his mind to be a little brat. Let him."

"You're asking me to give up on another human being? Where's your compassion, Kay?"

"Compassion is wasted on some people, John. Haven't you noticed?" I was still thinking of the Night Terror, and my anger had made me irrational. Of course Scott deserved our compassion. He was just a troubled kid.

John shook his head. "Not on Scott. I'm going to have a talk with his mother tonight. Scott has shown me a lot these last few weeks. He's not just hostile toward his mother, he positively despises her. Since it is socially unacceptable, not to mention illegal, to kill her and get that out of the way, he channels his anger through what he perceives as a macho form of release. Beating up other kids."

Times like this, I suspect John's getting his psychology degree from Phil Donahue University. "Is there anything you can do about that? I mean, if Scott doesn't like his mother, you can't change his feelings. Seems like a lost cause to me."

"There are no lost causes, Kay. Except me, perhaps. And a good woman could fix that."

"Are we back to your love life again?"

"To answer your question, I'm going to talk to Scott and, if I can, to his mother. She hasn't been especially interested in her son's problems before, but if I can help them reestablish a seminormal relationship it should help both of them."

"Well, good luck. Deep down, Scott's probably a fine young man. Are you sure he wouldn't like to come over one night? I could—"

"Positive," John assured me. "Eloise, put it on my tab." He shoved his plate out of the way and leaned across the counter to give her a peck on the cheek.

"You oughta marry this man, honey," Eloise said to me.

* * *

John offered to drop me off at the grocery store,
but I insisted that I wanted to get a bath and
change of clothes before shopping. The weather was
dry for February, and not overly chilly, so I felt
pretty darned righteous about getting my exercise,
too. I thought it might put an end to the guilt I felt
about my sedentary life. Which I'd have been perfectly happy with if friends, acquaintances, complete strangers, and the news media weren't always
telling me I'd be dead before I hit thirty.

I live in the first house on Morning Glory Way,
which is a one-way street going north. In order to
reach the grocery store, I could head straight up my
street, cross Main (which runs east and west), hang
a left through the connecting alley behind the
courthouse, and walk right through the door of
Hall's Market. Or I could take a left at Main, a
right onto Primrose (also a one-way, but running
south, parallel to Morning Glory), and reach Hall's
in the same amount of time. It's four-tenths of a
mile, either way.

And either way I'd pass the charred shell of the
Headlight office at the corner of Morning Glory and
Main. I always get a chill when I think of those innocent days at the paper. Oh, the job was terrific, but
it was during that time that Jesus Creek suffered
through a short and bloody spate of murders. And
just like they say, you never can tell about people. I'd
known the killer and never suspected a thing. Mild-
mannered and quiet. Most likely, people would say
the same thing about the Night Terror someday.

Stores and homes along my chosen route sported
limp yellow ribbons. The war in the Gulf had almost been forgotten, the prelude proving far more
exciting than the action itself. To my knowledge,
not one person from Jesus Creek had been shipped
off to the desert, nor had anyone mentioned relatives

involved in the war. We were patriotic enough to
hang up our flags, but beyond that, no one talked
much about the situation. I suppose others felt as I
did—if the apocalypse was upon us, there wasn't a
damn thing to be done about it. Might as well get
on with life.

Sarah Elizabeth Leach and her mother-in-law,
Eliza, were at the checkout counter in Hall's Market. From a quick glance at their purchases, I de-
duced that they had recently acquired a pet rabbit,
probably named Harvey. Eliza, as always, was brisk
and efficient, adding prices in her head faster than
the cash register could do it. Sarah Elizabeth looked
hungry.

"Hi, y'all," I said brightly, and selected a shopping cart with working wheels. I tucked my purse
into the section of the cart intended for toddler tot-
ing and began exploring my options.

The first aisle yielded two loaves of bread in
sturdy plastic packaging. Knowing that I'd never
find that French roast coffee John wanted, I didn't
bother to look. I just grabbed the cheapest brand
and threw it into the basket. The rest of the store
was equally uninspiring, so that by the time I was
ready to pay and leave, I had exactly the same items
I'd bought every week for years.

Connie, working checkout, greeted me profusely,
then launched into a rundown of all the news she'd
heard since my last shopping trip. Most of it concerned St. Pat's and the people who'd be arriving
for the celebration. She was able to fill me in on
travel plans for the entire community. No, she
hadn't heard any details about the corpse found in
the Host yard. Not yet, anyway. But she had several theories about the victim's identity, all of them
slightly ridiculous. Taking a moment to catch her
breath, she then went on to relate more immediate

news. "You know, Sarah Elizabeth was just here. That mother-in-law of hers is starving the poor girl to death."

"I know," I said, as I piled a few items on the counter. "She comes into the diner and eats like a lumberjack."

"No wonder. She's eating for two. You've never been pregnant, so you wouldn't know. But I'm telling you, Kay, those cravings drive a person nuts. The whole nine months I was carrying Billie Jo, I craved lemons! Sucked on 'em constantly. And with Becky Anne it was the strangest thing—exhaust fumes. I craved exhaust fumes! Nobody's ever been able to explain that one to me."

"I thought pregnant women craved foods that would provide nutrients their bodies were missing." Exhaust fumes, huh? That explained a lot about Connie, not to mention that fourth child of hers.

"Well, either way, Sarah Elizabeth is on a chocolate binge. We've worked out a way for her to just slip a few candy bars in her purse while Eliza's not looking, then Sarah Elizabeth pays for 'em the next day on her way to work."

"You mean old Eagle Eye Eliza hasn't noticed?"

Connie shook her head. "I distract her. You know, ask her some questions about one or the other of her relatives while Sarah Elizabeth grabs the candy."

"Think maybe Eliza needs to find a hobby?"

"She's got one: Sarah Elizabeth." Connie pushed a final button, and the total price of my week's groceries popped up in the little window at the top of the register.

"You're right. But Sarah Elizabeth may not be so easy to control. Eliza may have bullied the rest of her family into unnatural shapes, but she may have met her match this time."

While I wrote the check, Connie bagged the groceries, still explaining how Eliza wouldn't be so set on controlling Sarah Elizabeth if she'd had more than one child of her own. "An only child is a lonely child," she chanted. "And Lindsay James sure needed brothers and sisters. I'm glad I had all mine right together. Good for them, and believe it or not, easier for me."

"I'll take your word for it," I said, and grabbed a sack with each arm. "Personally, I don't plan to have children."

"Naturally not," Connie said. "Not until you find a husband."

I smiled and left, thinking that I probably should have reminded Connie that a husband, strictly speaking, wasn't necessary. But you just never know in Jesus Creek. Maybe she'd never heard that theory, and I didn't want to be the one to introduce her to it.

There are never makeup parties on Wednesday night. Everyone's in church. And no one needs a car washed in February. I suppose I could have walked some dogs for a little extra spending money, but I tried that once and swore off after Butch, the poodle, cost me forty-five dollars in lawn repair. So with John gone to save another disturbed child, I had the house to myself. That's pretty sad, isn't it? No one to call, no one to visit with. Even Bella was gone, running with the neighborhood cats, no doubt.

I took a shower and wrapped up in an old fuzzy robe, then stretched out on the couch with pen and legal pad to watch television and create poetry. Harder than it sounds. You see, poetry rules changed some time ago. Right after I learned to rec-

ognize a sonnet for Mrs. Crawford's English class,
in fact. Sonnets are out. No one writes them and
absolutely no one publishes them. So if you can't
tell a poem by its meter and rhyme, how is it dis-
tinguished from prose? Well, I'm not sure. I just
write sonnets, break up the lines in the middle, and
get lots of praise for my brilliant use of internal
rhyme from other poets but never from editors.

I'd rather be published than praised.

The news was still on and most of it seemed to
be the same stories I'd heard when I'd last checked
in. But the announcer devoted a full minute or so
to warnings about the Night Terror. (Could I write
a poem about the Night Terror? Possible title: "Terror Trembling.")

I listened patiently and composed the opening
line of my poem. *The dead and shadowed trees are
black* . . . I wondered if the Jesus Creek discovery
would be mentioned on the broadcast. The reporter
didn't seem to be getting to it in a hurry, so I added
a line to the poem— . . . *as depths/ of passion spent*
. . .—and considered calling the station myself.

When at last the review of criminal activity concluded and the real news began, I was stunned.
Cathy Ann Hopkins was a fraud!

"After several days of questioning by police, Ms.
Hopkins today admitted that she fabricated the
story of her abduction to get even with an ex-
boyfriend."

That put a new light on everything, didn't it?
We'd all gotten sidetracked by Cathy Ann's story,
and I had assumed the Night Terror was laying out
a complex pattern understood only by him. Now we
knew that wasn't true. With the discovery of the
body in Jesus Creek, we could now follow his prog-
ress in a near-straight line across the map.

He'd passed through Jesus Creek. I felt a jolt of

pure terror, thinking that he'd been that close. I could imagine his sitting around Eloise's after the murder. Hell, I could almost smell him. I desperately wanted to talk to someone I trusted. On the other hand, if I called anyone in town, we'd wind up talking about the murders, and that wouldn't make me feel any better.

I settled for pulling the phone closer to me (the better to dial 911 if the occasion arose) and sliding down to the floor in front of the sofa. That way I couldn't be seen by anyone peering through the windows.

I watched the rest of the newscast, hoping for information about the body Reb had found. All I got was the same story Henry Mooten had told and a promise of updates as soon as anything else was learned. And of course, I was reminded to avoid hopping in cars with strangers and to keep my vulnerable self locked up at home.

The movie that followed the news was called *Loved to Death*. It was about a seemingly gentle husband who slaughtered his succession of wives to collect their life insurance. I watched it because it was the best offering, and because I feel obligated to stay up late on Wednesday night since I don't have to work on Thursday. I finished the potato chips and pretended to revise the first two lines of my new poem. The evening dragged on until I was finally forced to admit that I was exhausted and needed sleep, never mind the freedom of off days.

John hadn't returned by midnight when I went to bed (without finishing the poem). Every creak the house made, every drip of the faucet, jerked me awake. Under the circumstances, I'd have been grateful for Bella's intrusive presence, but she'd evidently found better company for the evening; so I wound up staring at the ceiling until the wee hours.

CHAPTER
9

Strength, reversed: Discord creates fear; trust your knowledge.

THE AROMA OF FRYING MEAT WOKE ME BE-fore dawn. I may have had all of three hours of sleep, which was only a little better than none.

The layout of my house must have been intended to carry cooking odors into every room. Both bedrooms are at one end of the house, mine facing the street, John's facing the backyard. A two-foot square hallway connects those rooms to the living room and the kitchen. As an afterthought, the builder stuck a bathroom between John's room and the kitchen. And when John burns breakfast, I know it, no matter where I may be in the house at that moment.

I found him (John, not the builder) standing over the stove, frying bacon in one pan, frying eggs in another, and popping the last of twelve pieces of bread into the toaster. Bella was standing beside him, waiting patiently for her share of the food.

"It's four A.M.," I pointed out, with justified anger.

I poured myself a cup of the fresh coffee and slumped into a chair. But carefully, because I bought the dinette set at a yard sale two years ago and never got around to replacing the loose leg on one chair. Nor did I ever get around to disposing of, or at least marking, that chair. I just take my chances. It's my version of living life on the edge. "You know I don't eat anything until noon. My stomach can't take it."

"Okay, you caught me." He flipped an egg onto his plate. "I've been up all night with Scott and his mother, and I was starving by the time I got here. Sorry I woke you."

"Do you think your sob story can make up for my lost sleep? Because you're wrong." I refuse to apologize for being grumpy in the morning. It's a God-given right.

John piled toast and bacon onto the plate beside his eggs and made himself comfortable across the table from me. "Aren't you interested in why I was out all night? Didn't you even notice that I hadn't come home?"

"John," I said, with all the patience in the world, "you're always out late. If I worried about that, I'd be half-crazy by now." In truth, I felt a twinge of guilt about not having worried about him. Perhaps I'd been too concerned with my own safety. "But since I'm awake anyway, you might as well tell me what happened."

John continued to eat, but he managed to get most of the story out while he did so. "Scott wasn't home when I got there. Since he was expelled from school around ten yesterday morning, and since it was well past five before I got to his house, you can be sure his mother didn't know a thing about his latest escapade."

"Well, I suppose if I'd been thrown out of school, I'd be reluctant to tell my mother, too."

John nodded. "Of course you would. Even today, at your age. But right now we're talking about Scott. He's in bigger trouble than I thought."

"Really? He did more than hit another student, then." I was halfway through my cup of coffee and it still felt like four A.M. to me.

"Remember what I've told you about his mother?"

I nodded. "She's a drunken slut."

"That's what Scott had told me, and I foolishly believed him."

"Now you see?" I got up to refill my cup and tried to talk myself out of saying what I knew I was going to say. "I told you. You think everyone's mother is a drunken slut. So naturally you believed him."

"The fact is that she's a perfectly bland little woman who works at the shirt factory ten or twelve hours a day to support Scott and his sisters. The hovel that Scott keeps referring to is an average cracker box out on Dead Branch Road."

Dead Branch Road is one of the dead-end dirt roads that creep off the main highway here and there throughout Jesus Creek. For the most part, they're long driveways leading up to farmhouses. But once in a while, you come across the odd frame house tucked up in the middle of an old cotton field. Obviously, that was the sort of place where Scott lived.

"Everything the boy told me about his family is flat-out fabrication. Of course, his perception of the situation—"

"John, the kid lied. His perception can't possibly be that warped."

"All right, Kay. He lied. I admit that I was wrong."

"So what did you do? Stay there all night waiting for Scott to come home?"

"Course not. I had a long talk with his mother. She doesn't understand the seriousness of the problem. Tends to think of it as something teenagers do for fun, I guess. Or pretends she does. Classic denial. Anyway, Scott came in just as I was about to leave, around midnight. Needless to say, he was furious with me."

"Why would Scott be mad at you? You hadn't done anything."

"I'd done the worst thing imaginable. I'd caught him lying. There we all stood—Scott smelling of beer, his mother looking concerned and loving, and me, in Scott's opinion, shooting holes in his story. Which, naturally, he considers a betrayal of trust."

"His story was a lie," I pointed out. "How could he blame you for that?"

"He did. Just as he blames other people for his actions. We had a knock-down-and-drag-out. Scott was half-drunk, screaming and swearing and, every now and then, taking a swing at me. His mother was crying. Went on for about an hour before I was able to calm him down and talk sense to him."

"So now you think you've taught him to be a responsible adult?" I asked skeptically.

"I've at least gotten him to see that I'm his friend, even though I know he lied. He understands that I like him unconditionally."

I hoped John was right. Scott needed to know that someone cared for him, and John was the only person I knew with guts enough to stick by the kid through thick and thin.

"Anyway, I had a talk with his mother. Her name's Lola, by the way. She's concerned about

Scott. Knows some of what he's been into, but she hasn't a clue how to handle him. His father died four years ago. According to Lola, Scott had already started getting into trouble by then anyway—filching lunch money from other students, or tormenting the neighbor's cats. Standard behavior in these cases."

"Lola doesn't have blonde hair and blue eyes, does she?" I asked. "Maybe Scott's the Night Terror."

John looked up, as if amazed at my psychic powers. "Yes, in fact, she does have blue eyes. And sort of blonde hair. She doesn't bother to color it, but otherwise—"

"John, I get the idea. I'm serious now, though. You said Scott couldn't kill his mother because it's illegal. Don't serial killers always go after women who look like their mothers?"

"No," he said. "People kill for a variety of reasons. You'd need years of training to understand the motivation."

"Oh, right. And since you're trained, you have it figured out? If that's true, then why don't you geniuses put your heads together and catch the Night Terror?"

"Have you considered that he might be smarter than all the rest of us put together?" John jellied another piece of toast.

"If he's so smart, why doesn't he provide a useful service to humanity? No, I don't think he's all that bright."

"You're projecting again. Maybe he goes to work every day. And what does intelligence have to do with jobs? Or humanitarian services? For all you know, he might be secretly feeding the hungry every day."

"Who? Scott or the Night Terror?"

John raised his eyebrow, Spock fashion. "Maybe both."

I fell asleep on the couch while John was showering. When I woke it was almost nine-thirty and John, of course, was long gone. Off to the mines to unearth nuggets of gold from the souls of his students.

Dragging myself into the bathroom, I showered and shampooed. I reminded myself that this was the day I'd chosen to start my anti–Night Terror campaign. Somehow my goals had seemed much clearer the night before. In the harsh light of the bathroom's fluorescent bulb, I wondered what on earth I'd been thinking.

First of all, I couldn't very well enlist the women of Angela County to march through the streets armed with kitchen knives. Besides, Roger's army was already doing that. And what did I know about psychopathic killers, anyway?

There's nothing like a bright idea to get me going, and fortunately I'd just had one. The library would certainly have rows upon rows of books about crime and criminal behavior. I love it when adrenaline hits my brain. I was dressed, combed, and out of the house within fifteen minutes.

The library is practically across the street from my house, and I arrived just as Sarah Elizabeth was pushing open the lock with a screwdriver. (Don't ask. It's just the way we do things here.) She looked even larger than the day before, and I wondered if she might be hiding those chocolate goodies under her blouse.

"You look terrible," she said honestly.

"It's not noon yet, is it? Of course I look terrible."

Sarah Elizabeth giggled. "Great. Just what I

need—another grouch." She nodded in the direction of the office, where Pamela was bent over a ledger.

"We're thinking of declaring a holiday for grouches. Nominate her for committee chair. That should keep her busy."

Sarah Elizabeth rolled her eyes, as if to say she'd gratefully accept any reprieve from her assistant librarian. Unfortunately, Pamela decided to join us before we could get any sillier. One thing Pamela Satterfield does not tolerate is foolishness in the sacred reading room.

"I'll just look around," I said quickly, and dashed for the card catalogue before Pamela could offer to help. She doesn't much like patrons digging around in the shelves. Says they disturb the order of the books.

I was amazed at the number of crime-related books in the Jesus Creek library. Many of them were general studies of abnormal psychology and criminality, but I did find a couple that dealt specifically with serial murderers. I settled in at the circular table to read.

My first discovery was that there's a difference between mass killers and serial killers. The former take out several people in one whack, whereas the latter spread their victims out over a period of time. I pulled a small notebook from my purse and jotted this down. It seemed important to get my terms right if I wanted anyone to take my newfound expertise seriously.

Naturally, I had to slog through a lot of unnecessary information to acquire the facts I wanted, but by noon I had a long list of serial-killer traits. For instance:

1. Serial killers are most often white men in their twenties or thirties. I knew what John would say about that: the smart ones who don't get caught,

and therefore don't get entered into the statistics, are in their forties or fifties. You have to understand, John's pushing forty. He's grasping.

2. Stabbing often indicates a sexual motive for the killing. I shuddered at that one. We knew the Night Terror's victims had been stabbed. The police had revealed that detail, if nothing else. There'd been no mention of sexual abuse, though.

3. Many times the killers keep artifacts. I found it hard to believe that anyone with a working brain would be stupid enough to grab a murder victim's wallet and head home with it, but I kept that on my list, too. Someone ought to ask the police about this, I thought. They hadn't said a word about theft.

There'd also been rumors of mutilation, although, again, the police weren't being specific. One of the books I consulted listed mutilation as a sign of an organized murderer (as opposed to a murderer who kills in the heat of the moment). It also mentioned that moving the body is a sign of organization and planning.

So what I knew so far was that the killer was probably white, probably male, probably organized, and probably keeping souvenirs.

"What are you studying?" Sarah Elizabeth asked when she passed for the fortieth time.

"Murder," I said quietly, so as not to disturb the gray-haired couple working on their genealogy at the other side of the table.

"Good Lord. Don't you get enough of that from the news?"

"Yes," I confessed. "Do you have fresh coffee?" I stood up and stretched my arms above my head, trying to work the kinks out of my spine.

"Come on back. If Pamela says anything, I'll tell her you're my midwife."

Pamela doesn't believe that anyone should be in

the library office without an order from the president of the United States. Happily, Pamela is not in charge, and Sarah Elizabeth is getting tougher every day.

With our coffee mugs filled (and Sarah Elizabeth munching on a Mars bar), I explained my plan and revealed what I'd learned so far about serial killers.

"Roger Shelton collects those little cars," Sarah Elizabeth said facetiously.

"Yes, but I like Roger. Besides, if he's the killer, I'm sure he's only killing people who deserve it."

Sarah Elizabeth propped her feet on a spare chair. "I think this description fits most of the men in Jesus Creek, not to mention the rest of the world. Do you suppose there's a clue in the pattern?"

I nodded, eager to show off my knowledge. "Obviously. I figure the Night Terror must be incredibly methodical. Neat and precise. An accountant, maybe."

"Or Pamela," she whispered. "Why do you think that?"

"Well, just look at the trouble he's taken to leave victims fifty miles apart. And in a straight line across the state."

"If that's what he's up to, wouldn't he have started in Knoxville or Memphis, instead of in the middle of Tennessee? And what about Jesus Creek?"

"I give. What *about* Jesus Creek?"

Sarah Elizabeth sat up and plunked her swollen feet on the floor. "You mean you haven't heard about the body in Oliver Host's backyard?"

"Oh, sure. But that just proves my point. We were next in the line, like they'd been saying all along."

"No, Kay. Didn't you read this morning's paper?" Sarah Elizabeth reached behind her and plucked a Nashville paper from the counter. "The body they found in Oliver's yard isn't new. In fact, they suspect this victim may have been killed first. Before any of the others. So that means Jesus Creek wasn't next in line after Nashville—Jesus Creek was the beginning."

CHAPTER

10

The Hermit: Take time to become reacquainted with yourself.

"LET ME GET THIS STRAIGHT," ELOISE SAID, still holding the half-full coffeepot in front of her. "This killer started out by murderin' someone here in Jesus Creek, then he went off east somewhere and started leaving a trail of bodies behind him when he headed *back* here. Now what kind of sense is that?"

"Sense? You want sense?" I pointed to my empty cup to remind her why I was there. "I can only figure it means he's mapping out some kind of pattern. Not a straight line, of course, because he's ruled that out." I mused while Eloise made the rounds with the pot after filling my cup. The only idea that occurred to me was too horrible to contemplate for long: suppose the Night Terror was using Jesus Creek as a central point, a hub. If he started here, worked his way out and back . . . could he be planning to keep returning to

92

Jesus Creek before traveling west or north or south?

I sipped at my coffee. Somewhere in the back of my mind, I had this suspicion that the killer would pick up on my thoughts and actually start *doing* whatever I thought about.

After reading the newspaper article in the library, I'd hurried on down to Eloise's for lunch and a conference. Eloise is a remarkably wise woman, and I'd thought she might provide some insight. Unfortunately, I'd gotten there just in time to fight the lunch crowd. Needless to say, I felt so sorry for Eloise that I wound up helping serve, and by the time the majority of the customers left, I was starved and exhausted.

The coffee drinkers held up my lunch while they convened an impromptu meeting at the center table. I don't know if they'd contacted each other and planned it, or if fate had conspired to bring them all together. Either way, they were in session, and for a change they seemed more interested in discussion than coffee.

Anytime a town throws a party, there are always last-minute details that pop up. The St. Pat's parade, despite its history, was no exception. The problem of the day was a lack of green paint for the traditional St. Pat's Shamrock Trail that guided weary travelers into Jesus Creek. How would anyone find his way to the center of town if the shamrocks weren't painted on the parade route along Main Street?

"They're gonna sit their butts right there all morning," Eloise said, and propped herself on the counter. "Polishing chairs."

If Eloise had been in charge, the entire festival would have been planned down to the letter at least a month before. But the old-boy network thrived in

Jesus Creek. The mayor (a man, need I tell you?) chose one old boy to head the festivities, who in turn chose other men to head various committees. Those men chose still other men to serve on committees, with the occasional woman enlisted to do the dirty work.

Since my feminist sentiments aren't strong enough to induce me to complain, I held my seat and my mouth. I was too pooped to decide what I wanted for lunch.

"Well, it seems to me that somebody ought to be doing something," Eloise said. "Who *is* it that they found in Oliver's yard?"

"I don't know. Have you asked those guys?" I nodded toward the committee.

"Honey, they don't know dark from daylight. If they did, every one of 'em would be preaching the news at us. Reb hasn't been in, either. Never can find that man when you really need him."

"Shoot, Eloise. He wouldn't tell us anything. Has he given us one straightforward answer since all this began? Have any of them? I'm telling you, we've got to handle it ourselves."

"*We* as in *who*?" she asked.

"As in women. We're in danger, and all the police can advise us to do is lock our doors. Seriously. I think we should form our own watch club."

"Now, Kay, honey." Eloise gave me one of her mother-knows-best looks. "What do you have in mind?"

"I'm not sure what I have in mind," I answered honestly. "But, by golly, we've got to do something. When women can't go out alone for fear of being murdered, it's time to take action. All of us. We have to band together to protect ourselves."

"Kay, honey, that's exactly what they've been tellin' us to do. Stick together, don't go out alone."

Eloise shook her head, weary of the discussion. "Let me get you some food. Your blood sugar must be low." She sauntered into the kitchen and returned two minutes later with a plate full of the day's special: kraut and wieners.

"Pleasant conversation while you eat," she ordered. "Better for your digestion. You planning to dress up?" she asked me, then lit one of her long, skinny cigarettes.

"For St. Pat's? I thought I'd wear green, but damned if I'll deck myself out in body paint and curly-toed shoes."

"I bought myself a pair of green jeans and a spangly sweater to match. Jimmy's taking me out to dinner in Nashville after the parade, but I warned him, it'd better not be someplace so fancy I can't wear my St. Pat's jeans."

Jimmy is Eloise's son, hard as it is to believe. He's a chemical engineer, and his wife actually cross-stitched a pillow with the slogan A WOMAN'S PLACE IS IN THE HOME. Oddly enough, Eloise gets along beautifully with them both, but I suspect she prays every night that her grandson Jamie has inherited a few eccentric genes.

"You got a date for the picnic?" she asked.

I shook my head. "As soon as I finish work that day, I plan to go home. My idea of a perfect evening is to get to bed early. To *sleep*," I amended before Eloise could comment. "I've either been up late or up early the last three nights, and I'm ready to drop."

Eloise flicked her ashes into the plastic ashtray. "You're too young to be so dull."

"The other day you called me an old maid."

"Sex," Eloise said. "Perks you up, keeps you healthy and energetic. Try it."

"I don't think so. The nearest available partner

is John, and I'd hate to ruin a good friendship." I
wasn't about to admit that I'd considered the possibility. Eloise was so determined to add zest to my
life, she just might encourage him to court me. Now
John has many fine and desirable qualities, don't
get me wrong. But a codependent like me should
never, ever become emotionally involved with a recovering addict, no matter what the hormones say.
Since everyone alive today seems to be one or the
other, and since codependents are seldom attracted
to each other, my love life was looking damned dismal.

"There's that sweet Wayne Holland," Eloise
pointed out.

"I never date men who have more jewelry or hair
than I do." I reached up and patted my pixie hair-
cut for emphasis. "Even if I did, I'd want a long
chat with the ex-wife first. Just to get her side of
the story."

"Oh." Eloise blew out a puff of smoke with the
word. "I talked to my cousin Bill about that. Turns
out he knows Wayne pretty well. And everybody
over in Benton Harbor knows his ex-wife. They
generally refer to her as *that slut.*"

"Men!" I said, greatly disgusted. "They always
stick together."

"Actually"—Eloise arched an eyebrow—"it was
Bill's wife who mentioned it. And she's a friend of
the ex-wife's mother. Just so you'll know, his
mother-in-law sided with Wayne."

I was speechless. Was Eloise just making up un-
kind rumors about his ex-wife so that I'd go out
with the man? I wouldn't have put it past her. Or
could Wayne Holland be exactly what he appeared
to be?

"Fine," I said at last. "I'm willing to believe that
the divorce may not have been entirely his fault.

But I definitely am not looking for a man. Gary was trouble enough to last a lifetime."

Eloise practically sputtered with frustration. She jabbed out her cigarette in the ashtray. "Gal, I've got a long way to go with you." Starting for the coffee maker, she added, "I'll get you straightened out, though."

Before I could plead for mercy the front door opened and Roger Shelton burst in. Despite his habit of belting out love songs to Delia in public, he is not the hopeless romantic he seems. And so he sympathizes with my desire to be left unmated.

He normally sprawls out at a table, but noting the earnest expressions on the faces of the coffee drinkers, Roger wisely decided to sit at the counter. There he'd be relatively safe from any requests for assistance that the planning committee might have. While he'd thrown himself wholeheartedly into the statue project, he'd never shown any desire to work as part of a team.

"Where's Delia?" I asked, handing him a menu and grabbing an order pad from the counter. Reflex action.

"Cleaning house," Roger said gleefully, and leaned his elbows on the counter.

"And you don't do women's work, right?"

"Within reason. But Delia gets crazy every time her daughter comes to visit. Starts a month before to scrub the floors and dust the ceilings. She even makes me take all my clothes back to my house, so Charlotte won't, God forbid, think we're sleeping together." Roger rolled his eyes.

"Would Charlotte be upset?"

"Who knows? According to Delia, the kid is just looking for an excuse to lock up her mother in the attic." He glanced briefly at the day's handwritten lunch menu, then tossed it back at me. "Since I'm not being monitored by the Greenpeace guru, I'll have a hamburger steak. Rare. With bacon. And maybe a bowl of whale blubber for dessert."

When Eloise returned to the counter, I had Roger's order written up. She passed it on to Harry the cook and made a round with the coffeepot while entertaining the committee with suggestions for St. Pat events. (Something about strippers, which went over well until they realized she meant *male* strippers.)

"Eloise is trying to fix me up with a man," I told Roger. "Again."

He nodded sympathetically. "She can't help herself," he said. "Be patient with her, but be firm."

"You can count on it. This time she wants to pair me with that guy—you know the one. Ponytail."

"Wayne? He's got a steady job. No obvious physical flaws. Why don't you like him?"

"What?" I was stunned. In the time I've known Roger, I've never heard him speak well of anyone other than Delia. "Would you date a man with a ponytail and earring?"

Roger mulled it over. "Only if he had a great deal of money. Which he may have. You should find out."

"And why does everyone think he's so terrific? Divorces don't happen on their own, you know. Besides, y'all barely know him. You can't just assume—"

"I didn't realize you had such strong feelings about the man. Just forget I mentioned it."

"I don't have strong feelings. I'm trying to get the lot of you to understand that he's a complete stranger and we don't know diddly-squat about him. Also, I'm trying to protect myself from a bunch of would-be cupids, but I'm afraid—" Suddenly I ran out of words.

Seeing his chance, Roger jumped right in. "Afraid of what, Kay?"

Fortunately, Reb Gassler arrived at that very moment and joined Roger at the counter. "Hey, Rog," he said genially. It had taken awhile for Reb to warm up to Roger, probably because Reb long held an ember in his heart for Delia. But even Reb has been forced to admit that Roger and Delia are a perfectly matched pair, and he's begun to take a liking to Roger himself. "I see you've got a crew guarding that statue. I hope you've explained to them that guns aren't appropriate for the job."

"You don't think I'd let those clowns go near my statue with guns?" Roger sounded horrified. "I gave them a speech—darned clever one, too. I strongly urged them to use the good-old-boy approach to deal with trouble."

"What approach is that?" Reb asked.

"You know. Talk the culprit down."

"I believe that's what they do for people standing on ledges, Rog," Reb reminded him. "For potential statue thieves, the best strategy is to back off and let 'em go. Then give me a call and I'll just check around to see who's got the newest hernia."

"It's not thieves I'm worried about," Roger explained. "It's peekers."

Reb ordered chili before explaining the approved method of handling peekers, which involves bright lights and poison ivy. But never mind.

"Hear we had another fire last night," Eloise chipped in.

"You hear a lot, don't ya?" Reb winked. "Looks like we got a bunch of kids with time on their hands. The fire last night didn't do much damage, just threw a scare into the folks who woke up and smelled smoke in their living room."

Eloise served Reb's lunch and, oh so casually,

hung around the counter to make sure he had everything he needed. I decided to take my cue from
her and keep quiet until we got his stomach filled.

It took ten minutes before I asked the question
that was uppermost in my mind. "What's new on
the Night Terror?"

Reb looked at me and shook his head sadly.
"You're a morbid child. Like to visit the drunk tank
one night and watch 'em upchuck on themselves?
Or do you require blood and guts?"

"I'm not morbid. I'd just like to know he's been
caught. Have you identified the victim you found
yesterday?"

"Yep," Reb said, and crumbled a package of
crackers into his chili. " 'Fraid so."

He seemed to feel that was enough comment,
which forced me to ask, "Well, damn it, who is
she?"

"Nita Lowry," he said quietly.

I knew that Reb had dated Nita at one time, although I didn't think it had been a serious romance. Primarily because Nita had been married,
off and on, to Phil Lowry for the last ten years.

"Now wait a minute. The paper said this victim
had been killed weeks ago. How come none of us
noticed that Nita was missing?"

"Because Nita is missing half the time, Kay. She
has a fight with Phil, she takes off for a few days
or weeks—depends on the seriousness of the fight.
Even Phil didn't think it was odd this time. Poor
guy cried like a baby when he found out."

"Is he a suspect?" I asked.

"Everybody's a suspect." Reb went back to the
last of his chili and apparently felt our conversation had ended.

"Now, look, Reb. I've been doing some research

on serial killers. How much do you know about these people?"

Reb looked at me steadily. "Damn sight more'n I want to know."

That shut me up. I'd forgotten that he'd not only been close to Nita, but that he'd assisted at the crime scene the day before. Eloise jumped in to rescue us from the awkward silence.

"Do you think it's over now, Reb?" Eloise asked quietly.

"I don't know," Reb said. "But I don't recommend leaving your doors wide open. In fact, I don't even recommend inviting your best friends over to visit. According to what we've got so far, looks like the victims must have felt perfectly safe with this fella. Not a sign of a struggle anywhere."

"You mean they just smiled politely while he killed them?" I was flabbergasted.

"People don't expect to be victims," Reb said simply. "You see a buddy with bloody scissors in his hand. You assume he had an accident while cutting flowers or something."

"So the victims all knew the killer?" I reflected for a few seconds. "In all those different counties? Who gets around like that?"

"Some people do have social lives, Kay," Roger pointed out. "Why, I've heard of individuals who've had friends in different states, hard as that is to believe."

"Well, this Night Terror isn't going to have any friends left if he keeps this up, Roger," I said tartly.

"But he'll save a fortune on Christmas card postage."

In desperation I turned to Reb again. "And you can't predict if he's coming back to Jesus Creek?"

"I couldn't say. Tell you this, though, since you're clearly not gonna leave me in peace otherwise—far as we know, every victim has been traveling to or from work or school when last seen alive. One told her family she expected to meet a new friend after work and he might drive her home, but she didn't give his name and no one's come forward." Reb shook his head and smiled. "I believe I'll have a piece of that lemon pie for dessert."

"In a minute," I said. "Reb, I've been reading about serial killers. From what I've learned, it seems to me there must be more to this than you're telling us. We've all heard rumors about the bodies being mutilated, but what does that *mean*?"

Reb gave me a stern look and sighed. "You're gonna find out firsthand if you try to play cop."

"I'm *not* playing cop. Nor will you find me lurking behind bushes or wearing a trench coat. But I can't stand suspense. I'd feel a whole lot better if I had facts. The truth can't be any worse than what I've imagined."

"You want truth?" Reb asked. He stabbed at the pie I'd just placed in front of him. "Somebody's running loose, picking up women, stabbing 'em to death, chopping off body parts, arranging corpses in secluded—"

"Whoa! Chopping—?" I stopped, bloody visions twirling in my head.

"You said you wanted to know." Reb practically smirked. "Want me to tell you how it looks? Better yet, why don't I take you over to the office and show you the color pictures? Bet I could get you into an autopsy. That's real interesting." He filled his mouth with pie and went on. "Amazing how many critters you find crawlin' around in a body."

I chose not to pursue my line of questioning. Reb had already given me more information than I'd really wanted.

CHAPTER

11

The Wheel of Fortune: Begin by determining your own position, then set about designing your destiny.

IT WAS A FEW MINUTES AFTER THREE WHEN I got home and found Scott sitting on my front porch steps. Nothing could have pleased me more. (Yes, that's sarcasm.) After a long and frustrating day, I'd hoped for a hot bath, a quick dinner, and sleep. Instead I found myself wishing I'd cleaned house, even though Scott hardly qualified as company.

He was wearing jeans and a sweatshirt with the sleeves cut out, exposing his skinny brown arms. Scott would never be a husky man, nor a particularly tall one unless he was still waiting for his growth spurt. His expression didn't change when he saw me heading up the walk, but he did stand up to get out of my way.

"I was waiting for John," he said sullenly, as if I were to blame for John's absence.

"I expect he'll be here soon," I said lightly. "You can come on in if you like."

"Naw, shit. I'll head on out. He said he'd be here by now."

Having been stood up a few times myself, I knew how the boy felt, so I reached out and lightly touched his shoulder. "Look, John gets tied up at work sometimes. Why don't I wait here with you. He's bound to be in soon."

Scott mumbled something that sounded like an agreement and dropped back onto the steps. Pulling a knife from his pocket, he began to clean his grimy nails. This seemed to require substantial concentration.

I stopped short of sitting beside him, but I did put my purse down and take a deep breath of the fresh, mock-spring air. "Days like this make me wish for summer."

Scott didn't seem to care what I thought of the weather, and in fact his scowl suggested that he wished I'd go away. But I suspected that this was just part of his tough-guy act. No doubt he wanted me to stay and keep him company until John returned. I figured I could handle that.

"I see you've got your bike out today. I guess this is ideal weather for riding."

Scott glanced out toward his motorcycle, parked by the curb. "I've been down by the creek," he said.

"Must be chilly by the water. Don't you get cold in that shirt?"

He scowled a little harder, and I realized I'd probably sounded just like a mother. "Somebody's moved into the Tyler house," he offered.

"Really? I didn't think they'd ever sell that place. It's been empty so long that people claim it's haunted. You know, I've heard stories about ghostly lights being seen there late at night—"

"Bunch of shit," Scott commented mildly.

"Well, yes. I expect it is. Do you know who bought it?"

He shook his head in one brief, jerky movement. "Just somebody from out of town. No big deal."

"Whoever it is, I hope they'll fix the old place up." The Tyler house is a monstrous Victorian dwelling that could pass for an Alfred Hitchcock set. It sits up on a hill overlooking the creek. Perhaps *looms* would be more accurate. "The new owners aren't named Bates, are they?"

Scott missed my attempt at levity. "Naw. I don't know the last name. I just talked to Dave a little bit. He's the guy that bought it." He snapped his knife shut and slid it back into his pocket.

"Oh," I said. I wondered if Scott was the only Jesus Creekian Dave had met. If so, the Tyler house might be empty again soon.

Silence passed between us like a hippo moving through mud. Finally, for my own comfort, I tried a new topic. "John tells me you're a terrific mechanic. He says you keep the motorcycle running all by yourself." Didn't *I* sound like a cheerleader?

"I'm pretty good at it," he admitted. "I'd rather have a car."

"I suppose you could buy an old one for next to nothing. Since you're good with motors, I'll bet you could get any old lemon to run."

"Can't afford to buy one, not even a junker."

I realized that he had a valid point there. I was a grownup with a full time job, and I couldn't afford a car either. Bella wandered around from the side of the house and trotted over to rub her head against my leg. The whole time she was eyeing Scott, and when she'd had her fill of me (which didn't take long), she moved smoothly over to him and crawled up into his lap.

Scott patted her once absently, and Bella moved

on, across the yard and into the neighbor's territory. "Do you have a summer job lined up?" I asked, still thinking that maybe we could figure a way for him to get a car.

"Naw. Nothing to do around here. Besides, even if somebody had a job, they wouldn't give it to me. Ya gotta know people to get on. And I'm not sucking up to nobody just for a two-bit paper route in this slime hole."

Well. Clearly Scott was not interested in just any sort of employment. At first glance, this would appear to be a personality problem, I thought. On the other hand, it could indicate that he's set his goals high and intends to meet them.

"What sort of work would you *like* to do?" I asked, genuinely interested.

John's car rumbled into place by the curb and drowned out any answer Scott might have ventured. We both waved, no doubt equally relieved to have John's intervention in our decidedly strained conversation.

Casually, like a man who'd just assembled all the suspects at the end of the play, John sauntered up the walk toward us and greeted Scott. He didn't bother to say hello to me, but I didn't feel that was the time to correct his manners.

"Come on in, Scott," he said. "Have you had dinner?"

Charming, I thought as I followed them inside. Invite the boy to eat. And don't bother to hold the door for me or anything like that, because I am a liberated female with highly developed skills of survival. I can open my own doors. But they'd better not ask me to cook, I added to myself.

"Coffee's ready," John told me as I rummaged through the cabinets and fridge for food. "Sorry I

interrupted your chat. You two just go on like I'm
not here."

Knowing that John was not sincere (he doesn't
like conversations that don't include him), I made
no effort to continue discussing Scott's job options.
Instead I handed the boy a coffee mug from the collection hanging on the wall.

Scott watched as John filled his cup. "I'd like
something a hell of a lot stronger."

"Of course you would." John said it in such a
way that it made Scott seem a foolish child. "But
coffee is all we have at the moment."

Scott glared at me. The boy seemed to think I was
responsible for every inconvenience in his life.

"Scott and I have been discussing the problems
at school," John explained.

"That bastard Williams," Scott muttered.

"Who's Williams?"

"The principal," John explained. "He and Scott
have some trouble relating to each other."

"He's gonna be the one with trouble." Scott had
clearly been watching tough-guy movies. He'd mastered the talk. Now if only he could grow several
inches and gain fifty pounds, he might sound convincing.

"I understand that you feel he's being unreason-
able," John said. "And perhaps he is. But like it or
not, he's the boss. For now."

"He's not *my* goddamned boss," Scott insisted.

I wondered if Scott had ever had his mouth
washed with Ivory but decided he probably hadn't.
No doubt his colorful language was used only
around his buddies. Like John. Which led me to
wonder if John's attempts to be the boy's friend
were wise.

"He *is* your boss, Scott," John went on. "Look,

here's the way it works. High school is a conspiracy."

Scott looked up sharply, probably surprised to hear any adult speaking blasphemy. But at least John seemed to have captured his attention.

"That's where they weed you out. You think those teachers want you to learn? Think again, boy. The object is to wear you down. To dump as many of you as possible. We don't want every single one of you going on to get advanced degrees. Hell, who'd pump gas and dig ditches?" John never cracked a smile. Sometimes I wonder just how well adjusted *he* is.

Scott thought it over for a while, then said, "Shee-it!"

"Whatever you say." John leaned back in his chair far enough to grab the coffeepot from the counter and refill his cup. "But keep it in mind. Watch. See if you can find any evidence to the contrary. I can't swear to this, but I'd be willing to bet there's a list somewhere in Williams's office. I think they keep up with the students least likely to do well, like you. And then they start pounding away, trying to make you flunk out or, even better, quit school. Then they can cry and moan and carry on about the dropout rate and those poor children who never had a chance because they lack education."

Scott was quiet. Well, after all, what could he say? He'd just discovered that his guidance counselor was a lunatic.

"So what the hell am I bothering for?" Scott finally burst out. "If the whole damn world's out to get me?"

"Because you can play the game, that's why. But you have to, one, know the rules, and two, play by your own. They just hate when that happens." John smirked.

"Shit, no! I'm not suckin' up to Williams or any-body else."

"Think, boy! You've got the knowledge to thwart them now. You know what they're up to. Once you know it's a game, you've got a chance to win it! You can make up your own rules, play it your way. But the key is to let them *think* you're giving them what they want."

By this time, I was completely fascinated by John's tale. I don't know how he comes up with this stuff, whether he makes it up on the spur of the moment or stays awake nights composing it. John and Scott were staring each other down when Bella wandered in. They didn't even notice the plump lit-tle mouse that she dropped on the floor at my feet.

"I'll make more coffee," I offered. I didn't really want to, but there seemed a need for a brief respite, and John and Scott were both too caught up with excitement to call a break.

I ran water into the pot and watched the two of them glare at each other for a minute. Without tak-ing his eyes off the boy, John pulled the tarot deck from his shirt pocket. "Reading?" he offered.

Scott nodded and held out his hand to take the pack. He shuffled and cut the cards with a sureness that told me he'd done this many times before. I wondered briefly if John did readings for all his stu-dents. If so, the parents would be pounding on our door one of these days and demanding to know why John was teaching their children satanic arts.

While waiting for the coffee, I leaned over John's shoulder and studied the cards spread across the table. Even with my limited knowledge of the tarot, I could recognize trouble when I saw it. Most of Scott's cards indicated misfortune, failure, foolish-ness, and arguments. I wondered if he'd go right out and rob a gas station when John told him.

Apparently Scott knew even less about the cards than I did, because he accepted what John told him. And John lied.

"Here," John said, pointing to the reversed Fool card. "You've had a decision to make, either in the immediate past or in the present. If you've thought it over carefully and chosen the sensible path, you're going to do well. That might relate to what we've just been talking about."

Well, okay. I suppose the card could have meant just that. But John went on with positive interpretations throughout the reading, and I knew I couldn't have been mistaken about every card.

The resolution card was the biggie as far as I was concerned. That's the last card in the spread, and it rounds out the other cards. Looking back at what you've learned from them, the resolution is a predictor. Most of us, of course, just want to hear about that one card, because it tells the future. Oh, John and the other tarot readers will get all iffy about it and say it merely suggests what *could* happen. But I figure they're trying to avoid bad karma or something. Trust me. It predicts the future.

Now Scott's resolution card was the Two of Cups, reversed. And I knew flipping well it meant he'd go on being argumentative and disruptive until somebody finally bashed his mouth for him. But John, good old John, wasn't going to tell the kid that.

"You need to work at relationships," he said. "One in particular, the one we've been discussing throughout this reading. It can be saved, and even valued, if you work at making it right."

Scott stared out the window and seemed to be considering what John had just told him. I thought his face looked a little softer than I'd ever seen it, and his eyes were kinder for just a moment. Then he pulled himself together and slipped back into his brat persona.

"Yeah, thanks," he said without feeling. "So you're saying I gotta do all the work. If I give in to Williams and to my old lady and to you"—he pointed a finger at John—"then *maybe* you'll all let me alone."

"Is that how you interpret the reading?" John asked.

"Shit, yeah. Don't you?"

I was beginning to wish someone would teach that boy a new obscenity.

"Coffee?" I asked, as the pot finished gurgling.

"Don't bother," John said, and glanced at his watch. "It's late. Scott needs to get home before his mother calls out the rescue squad." He dismissed Scott that simply, and the boy left through the back door without saying goodbye.

I thought Scott was a hopeless case, but I had to admit that when he'd heard John talk about school being a game, there had been light in his eyes that looked curiously like joy. Maybe John was more resourceful than I thought. I wondered if Scott was going home now to consider what John had said about the tarot cards. It could be, I thought, that John really is turning the boy around.

CHAPTER

12

Justice: Do not cling to mistaken ideas.

JOHN HAD FINISHED OFF THE LAST OF THE bread, but hadn't bothered to remove another loaf from the freezer. He never does. I tossed the empty wrapper to him, hoping he'd feel at least a little guilty about the fact that I'd have to eat my bologna on toast. He just folded the plastic into a neat square and stuck it in his back pocket, then pulled the tarot pack from his shirt pocket and began shuffling.

"Is that reading for you or me?" I asked.

"Would you like a reading?" He held the deck out to me, but I shook my head.

"Whatever the cards say today, I expect I'd be sorry to learn it." The truth was, I'd grown tired of vague predictions and attempts to unravel my neuroses. Sometimes I wished John would take up a new hobby. Something that didn't affect me. Bowling maybe. "I learned something from Reb today. The Night Terror mutilation? Reb says he's cutting off body parts."

John's eyebrows rose a half inch, and I could see I had his full attention. "Which parts?"

"I forgot to ask."

"You forgot?"

"I know, I know. But it threw me, and then Reb started carrying on about autopsies and other disgusting subjects. I don't want to discuss this while I eat."

"We can continue in the car then. You've only got an hour, though," he reminded me.

"Until what?"

"Until we leave for the meeting. Or are you planning to skip it again?"

John was not pleased with my absence from the last few twelve-step-program meetings. I know regular attendance is strongly suggested, but I figured John was going enough for both of us.

"I feel like road kill." No way would he fall for that one, so I rushed on. "And lately I haven't felt especially elated after the meetings, either."

"Could be your attitude," he said smugly.

"Or it could be that I've been going so long I've heard all there is to hear. Maybe it's time I started doing more than just listening." I put a piece of bologna in Bella's food dish, which she promptly snatched up and carried into the living room.

John turned in his chair to look at me. "What do you think you should be doing?"

I slapped my sandwich together and carried it to the table, trying to decide how to answer him. "I'm not sure. But the problem is, I feel like I'm wandering around with all these words in my head. I'm full of good advice. But it's empty, you know? *This* is how I'm supposed to feel. *That* is what I'm supposed to say." I shook my head. "It just doesn't happen. I don't feel any better about

Gary, or about myself, or about the way my life is
going."

For a moment I thought John would ask another
of his textbook questions, but he surprised me by
leaning forward and looking at me with obvious
concern. "You should feel very good about yourself,
Kay," he said evenly. "You're a wonderful woman."

"Oh, yeah? Then why don't I have a life? I mean
a real life?"

"Maybe you haven't been looking in the right
place," he suggested. "Or at the right goals. What
do you want, Kay?"

I opened my mouth, but nothing came out. Probably because my brain had just gone dark. I wanted
to be deliriously happy, no question about that. I
suppose that was the first time I'd ever thought
about it, though. My approach to life is a mellow
one. I've always tried to stay out of trouble, get
through the days with a minimum of fuss, and avoid
a tax audit. Is that asking for too much?

John was still sitting there, waiting for me to answer. Finally I said, "I don't know, John. I don't
have a name for what I want."

He reached across the table and patted my hand,
then rose and began getting ready for the meeting.
He must have realized that he'd flipped a switch
inside of me, because he didn't say another word
until he was ready to leave.

"You're not demonstrating beauty products tonight, are you?" he asked when he came out of the
bathroom.

"No. Seems like my bookings are awfully slim
these days. Of course, just about everybody in town
has already had a party. I don't know, John. You
think maybe I'm not cut out for this business?"

"I'm sure of it. But things happen as they should.

If you get tired of pitching makeup, you'll be forced to find something you enjoy doing."

"Like marrying into the Royal Family? Those positions are filled."

John gave me a genuine smile. "You'll be a queen when you find that King of Cups. How's he doing, by the way?"

"Are you still pretending that I've got a chance at romance? Grow up, John. These days I couldn't date a man if I found one. You never know anymore who'll turn out to be a killer."

"You've heard about Nita Lowry?" he asked.

"Uhm-hmm. I didn't know her very well. Did you?"

John downed the last half of his coffee. "Yes, I did. She worked at the school. Secretary. Nice woman, too."

"Reb used to date her once in a while. He seems pretty upset about her death. Well, of course, it's hard to tell with Reb. He'd not exactly open about his feelings."

"That's a plus in his job. Nita's body was badly decomposed by the time Reb saw it."

I'd never seen a decomposed body, so I couldn't have imagined what it looked like even if I'd wanted to.

"I'm sorry about Nita. Friends aren't easy to come by. It's a shame you've lost one."

He nodded. "You're right."

Once John was gone I regretted not having accompanied him to that meeting. But I convinced myself that here was a golden opportunity to finish the poem I'd been working on. It had ceased to be about the Night Terror. I'd decided that it really described an empty life.

And so I continued. *The dead and shadowed trees*

*are black as depths/ of passion spent. A film of an-
guished moon/* . . . Well, maybe *depths* wasn't the
right word. Words did not come as easily as they
might have—the upshot of sleep deprivation, I concluded.

I began to doodle on the edge of the paper. I made
warped maps of Tennessee and tried to put dots in
the places where the bodies had been found. I
wound up drawing circles around the dot that rep-
resented Nita Lowry.

Nita had been one of those women you knew
about even if you didn't *know* her. She'd moved to
Jesus Creek sometime after her marriage, I supposed, because I had a vague idea that she'd grown
up in Benton Harbor. Attractive woman, in an obvious sort of way. Lots of auburn hair that framed
a sweet, but overly made-up, face. I'd chatted with
her around town but never had a conversation with
her.

The poem I'd been writing became a eulogy for
Nita. I worked on it for several hours until I had it
in reasonably good shape, then decided to tidy it up
the next day. It made me feel better to think that
I'd made a gesture to mark her absence.

I was grateful for the opportunity to sleep without Bella's claws digging into me. Ordinarily she
likes to curl up on top of the covers, shifting and
scratching until she's comfortable, but she hadn't
yet returned from her nightly hunting expedition.
Unfortunately, I tossed and turned for at least an
hour anyway, trying to think clearly about the subject John had brought up earlier. And failing.

I'd just realized that all my energy had been put
into avoiding unpleasantness. The path of least re-
sistance—that's the rule by which I'd lived. And it
wasn't working. Having decided that the hollow-
ness inside was caused by a lack of enthusiasm for

my life, I vowed to isolate at least one thing that would bring me joy and set about naming it the next morning.

Eventually I drifted off, and would no doubt have awakened bright and chipper after a refreshing sleep if I'd been allowed to do so. Instead, I was roused just past midnight by a relentless scratching on my front door. "Only this and nothing more." Right.

I crawled out of bed, getting entangled in the sheets and ending up on all fours on the floor. Assuming that Bella was too lazy to go around back and crawl through the cat door John had installed, I didn't bother to search for a robe. No one was likely to be passing by the house at that hour anyway, and my flannel gown is modest attire. I wasted considerable effort swearing as I made my way through the hall and living room to the door.

Even my sleep-fuzzed brain was wise enough to remind me to look before opening, which I did. And saw not a soul outside on the porch. I stumbled through the house to the back door and peeked out. No one.

Convinced that I'd dreamed the noise, I swore again and scurried back to my bed, but it took another half hour to get comfortable enough to fall asleep. And of course, during that time, I was again plagued by thoughts running rampant through my head. The last one that I remember had to do with elective surgery, the plan being to get a long sleep in the recovery room.

Breakfast was, as usual, a cup of John's coffee. I always managed to find time for toast or cereal at the diner, and would have skipped even coffee at home except that John always had it ready. I can't say that I'd ever known him to sleep, although he must have been catnapping somewhere along the way.

"I'm going to drop from exhaustion," I told him as I stumbled into the kitchen, still in my gown. I took the mug that John offered me and draped myself across a chair. "It's some form of conspiracy. The universe is determined that I will not be allowed to rest."

"Paranoia isn't becoming," he said, and handed me a cup of coffee. "You had the house to yourself last night. Why didn't you go to bed early?"

I growled and glared, but John has gotten used to that. "In the middle of the night, just as I was getting into some quality sleep, somebody came pounding on the door. Well, scratching or rattling or something. At any rate, it woke me."

John was slathering jelly on his six pieces of toast and didn't seem at all surprised by my tale.

"When I opened the door, there was no one there!" I finished.

"Maybe you dreamed it." Having loaded his plate with toast and eggs, John joined me at the table. "Your subconscious is trying to tell you something."

"Oh yeah? Like what?"

"Knocking. Opportunity knocks, or so they say."

"They say it knocks once. This was a series of noises, not knocks."

He didn't answer, but I pondered it some more while I dressed. Just before I'd fallen asleep, I'd been trying to decide what I should do with my life. Maybe my subconscious *had* been talking to me. If so, did my dream mean that the time was right to make changes? Was today the day that I would reach a turning point in my life? Would it all be made clear?

By the time I'd finished dressing, I was feeling

downright chipper. Giddy, in fact. The more I thought about it, the more likely it seemed that life was about to blossom with the promise of a glowing future.

I rejoined John at the table to finish my coffee. "Mind if I take the paper?" I asked, reaching for *The Benton Harbor Sun*.

"Be my guest," he said, seeing that he had no choice. "But you're not going to like it."

"Why?" I asked naively, and began skimming the front page. The lead story was about the Night Terror, of course. Somehow they'd managed to include the information about Nita's body being found. (Ordinarily the paper's deadline is Wednesday and it comes out on Friday. Nita had only been identified the day before, but someone was on the ball.) "Oh, my Lord," I said, taking a gulp of coffee. As if I thought caffeine would make the situation more bearable.

"Told you." John took the paper away from me and dropped it on the floor beside him.

At last the authorities had decided to share a few more details with the general public, no doubt in desperation. Clearly they weren't getting anywhere with this investigation. The Night Terror, it seemed, had indeed been keeping souvenirs.

"I can't believe this," I said between gasps. "That's disgusting."

"It's not so unusual. Besides, Reb has already warned you about it."

"I know," I said. "He wasn't this graphic. Do you mean to tell me that the man is just going around, killing women and cutting off their fingers to keep as mementos?"

"No," John said, straight-faced. "Memen-*fingers*."

I felt a rush of fury and almost slapped him.

"That's not funny. How can you possibly joke about something so vicious? Your friend, Nita . . ."

"Yes, I know," he said, somewhat chastened. "I'm sorry. Black humor is my forte. I forgot that it's not yours."

"You should be sorry. I don't care how many serial killers are running loose in this country, or how many people they kill. You can't lump the bodies together and call them statistics. Each and every death is a tragedy. And you can't read this"—I shook the paper at him—"and call it typical behavior in a murder of this sort. It's desecration and it's humiliation, not just another clue!"

John reached across the table and put his hand around mine on my cup. "I'm sorry," he repeated. "I truly didn't mean to upset you."

I pulled my hand away and stood up. "I'll make dinner tonight," I said as I made a final pass through the house on my way out the front door.

While I gathered my purse and jacket, I tried to wipe the image of Nita's mutilated body from my mind. I chanted to myself, over and over: it's going to be a beautiful day, it's going to be a beautiful day. . . .

And then I opened the front door and felt my stomach drop into my feet.

The noise that I'd heard the night before had not been a late visitor trying to get my attention. It had instead been the sound of a knife of some sort, etching a design into my front door.

"It's a pentagram," John said quietly.

"I know that!" I snapped. "Did you read the message?"

Carved into the door, just above the crude pentagram, were the words YOU NEXT.

"That's what you heard last night," John said unnecessarily.

"Was it him?"

John knew whom I meant. "No, of course not. There's been no mention of anything like that from the Night Terror."

"Well, there's been no mention of missing fingers until this morning, either," I shot back. I was not feeling kindly toward the police or any other officials who'd decided to keep the public in the dark about the Night Terror's signature.

"You know what's happened?" John said with false cheer. "Someone hit on the idea of stirring people up, that's all. You've heard about copycat killers and professional confessors. Someone just thought it would be cute to pull a stunt like this. Probably left the same calling card all over town last night."

"Really?" I wanted to believe it. That note—YOU NEXT—in light of all that had happened, was enough to turn my very bones to ice. But if other women had it carved into their doors, I didn't have to take it personally.

"This is just a rougher version of toilet paper in the trees. You're far too sensitive."

"Like hell I am!" I may have been hysterical, but I wasn't stupid. "Somebody went to a lot of trouble to put that there. And it was meant to scare me. You bet I'm sensitive."

"Most likely it was some demented psycho who picked our house at random. People do things like this, Kay. For no reason except that they do."

It didn't make a lot of difference to me if I'd been chosen at random or not. My point was that someone had been out there, on my porch, engaged in an activity designed specifically to terrify me. And he'd probably been there somewhere when I opened the door the night before.

"I was standing there in my gown!" I wailed, which mystified John, since he hadn't been privy to my train of thought.

"You need coffee," he said sternly, and pulled me from the chair. "Come on. I'll pour."

I followed him meekly into the kitchen. Clearly he wasn't taking this to heart. But I had just made the connection. Pentagrams and human fingers. The Night Terror had to be a demented cult member. This possibility did nothing to alleviate my anxiety.

CHAPTER
13

The Hanged Man, reversed: You cling too much to the past and thus waste energy.

JOHN MADE FRESH COFFEE AND BROUGHT me toast, which I couldn't eat. He chatted inanely in an attempt to convince me that the sunshine was still as bright as it had been earlier. When that didn't work, he urged me to express my feelings. For the record, I felt frightened.

Curled up in a living room chair, I continued to insist that wood carving was not a craft one practiced on random doors. There was absolutely no doubt in my mind that I'd been singled out for harassment. John told me I was overreacting.

"This happens, Kay," he kept saying. "Every now and then a pocket of would-be satanists decide they're tired of dancing around in the woods."

"Exactly. And then they start murdering women. Have any of the news reports mentioned the victims receiving warnings?"

He shook his head, obviously convinced that I

wasn't going to be reasonable. And I darned sure
wasn't.

"I'm calling Reb," I said, rising from the chair.
"I want someone to know about this. Besides, just
because we haven't heard of it happening to anyone
else, doesn't mean it hasn't. Reb is so damned close-
mouthed about the Night Terror—"

John sighed. "At the risk of encouraging you, I
think that's a good idea." He returned to the
kitchen, undoubtedly to make yet more coffee, while
I made the call. But first I checked in with Eloise
to let her know I'd be coming in late.

Reb was having his breakfast, the dispatcher told
me, but she interrupted him and he arrived on my
front door step approximately fifteen minutes later.
I made John answer the door.

"Damned shame," Reb said after we'd told him
what happened. He surveyed the door carefully and
even checked the porch and the ground outside for
evidence. He found nothing but the raw scars in my
door. "Some people ought to be hung up by their
. . . thumbs. Look at that," he said with disgust.
Pointing to the door, he traced the pentagram with
his forefinger and shook his head. "Good workman-
ship in these old houses. I'll bet you won't be able
to replace this with anything half as sturdy."

I suggested we adjourn to the kitchen table for
coffee before Reb became totally enamored with my
woodwork. Since John and I drink our coffee black,
I'd had to scramble through the cabinets in search
of sugar for Reb. While I was doing that, the two
men had carefully avoided mentioning the reason
Reb was there, in a misguided attempt to make me
forget about it myself. Fat chance.

"It really scares me, Reb," I said, with only a
touch of whine in my voice. I plunked the sugar
bowl down in front of him and slid into a chair.

"Somebody did this on purpose. Did it to *me* on purpose."

John started to protest, but Reb beat him to it. "Who on earth would want to harass you, Kay? Unless you're leading a double life, I can't imagine a soul who doesn't want the best for you." He waited patiently while I wrestled with a reply.

Not that I'm loved and adored by everyone I meet, you understand. There are some people in Jesus Creek who wouldn't give me the time of day. But I couldn't imagine any of them going out of their way to *tell* me they don't like me. Especially not in such an artistic way.

"Look on the bright side, Kay," John said suddenly. "Maybe it was someone with a grudge against me."

Reb and I looked at him expectantly, but John seemed to have nothing else to say.

"Who'd hate you that much?" I asked.

John leaned back in his chair and smiled. "Three ex-wives," he said, counting them off on his finger, "innumerable students, employers, landlords, relatives—"

Reb jerked his thumb toward the front door. "How many of 'em are weird enough to do something like that?"

"I'll tell you who'd do it," I snapped. "The same sort of person who'd kill women and drop them off in Oliver Host's yard. It's a satanic symbol. They pride themselves on their evil ways, don't they? Well, it seems to me it would take a core of pure evil to make a man capable of serial murder."

"Not evil, necessarily," John said. "Sometimes it's just confusion or pain." Finishing the last drop of coffee, he stood up and stretched slowly. "Keep the doors locked, Kay. Take sensible precautions, and forget this incident as quickly as you can. My students are expecting me to give them a test today, or I'd stay here with you."

"How am I supposed to ignore it? Every time I enter or leave the house I'll be reminded that someone's out there waiting to kill me." I'll admit I was somewhat shrill, but I figured, since no one else was taking it seriously, I'd better complain all I could before I wound up dead.

"I know you're scared." John knelt on the floor beside me and took my hand in his. "But you can't lock yourself up here and whimper all day." He chucked me under the chin like I was a pouting child and said in an appeasing voice, "I absolutely guarantee that you haven't been targeted."

Once John had exited the room, I turned to Reb and demanded the truth. "Has this happened to the Night Terror victims? Did they receive warnings before they were murdered?"

"I haven't heard if they have. But I'll check with the TBI soon as I get back to the office. You gonna be here awhile? I'll call and tell you whatever I've learned."

"They'd have mentioned it to *you*, surely. John's right, isn't he? I'm overreacting. This isn't the Night Terror, it's just some nut with time on his hands."

I looked up at Reb for confirmation, but he only shrugged.

Word travels at light speed in a small town. Delia Cannon called before I could pull myself together and leave for work. She sounded genuinely worried on my behalf, and genuinely disturbed by what she and I both felt was a significant act of evil.

"Is John there with you?" she wanted to know.

I told her he'd been a rock, trying valiantly to calm my fears. "In fact, I'm seriously considering bearing his children," I said, and tried a casual chuckle.

"Well, he is a good-looking man," Delia said.

Reb called just after that. "Kay," he said, sounding grim, "I can tell you absolutely that not one of the Night Terror victims has had a pentagram engraved on her door."

"I don't like the way that's worded, Reb. Did anyone receive a warning of *any* kind?"

There was an instant's pause. "Not that I know about. I'll keep checking. Meanwhile, you keep yourself safe." He hung up before I could ask for more reassurance.

After that, I got three more phone calls in rapid succession. By the time I'd finished telling my story and wallowing in pity, it was almost eleven and I felt somewhat better. Well enough, at any rate, to remember that the electric bill needed to be paid, so I checked all the locks and went to work by way of my back door.

The diner was almost empty, except for a few straggling coffee drinkers, but I knew that Friday lunch was upon us. Without stopping to listen to Eloise carry on about how I needed to stay at home and rest, I hustled around the room, setting up menus, building a pile of napkins and utensils to hand out, and generally making myself useful.

Because it was Friday, and the lunches lasted longer than usual, it was almost dinnertime before the crowd thinned out. I'd been asked more than once about my experience of the night before, but fortunately I was too busy for embellishments. Halfway through the rush, I realized that any one of those curious customers might be the Night Terror.

I glanced at Benny and Chester, seated snugly at their favorite table. Two doddering old men who

spoke little, smiled less, and appeared in town only
at mealtime. Oddball personalities if any existed.

But I quickly realized that I'd get nowhere trying
to decipher personalities. Over in the corner, Frank
Pate was trying on his green top hat. The color had
faded and it no longer matched the green tights he
wore. Beside him sat Henry Mooten, a man who'd
tied a green ribbon to his emergency earthquake
survival kit in celebration of the upcoming holiday.
And just entering the room was Will Davis. Will
had appointed himself chief of security in charge of
maintaining the secrecy surrounding the identity
of the grand marshal.

Face it, I told myself: everybody in this town
could cop an insanity plea.

And because it was Friday, I had no particular
plans for the evening. No one books a party on Friday night. I suppose they think other people might
have something else to do, although I can't imagine
what those plans would be.

Jesus Creek's recreational opportunities are limited to The Drink Tank, a sleazy bar serving beer
and cheeseburgers, and The Video Arcade, which
caters primarily to teenagers. Adventurous folks
will drive into Nashville for a movie and a saunter
through Shoney's salad bar.

Even after a shortened workday, I was looking
forward to a long, hot, scented bubble bath, a sandwich in front of the television, and conversation
with John—if he wasn't off to another meeting. My
earlier resolve to improve my life and create my
own opportunities was gone. The effort seemed
greater than the reward.

Outside, the sky had been clouding up all afternoon in concert with the weatherman's promise of
an all-night rain, and my main concern was getting
home before the storm broke. I wanted to be safely

tucked away with all the lights on before the thunder started crashing.

Eloise was taking a break at the family table and chatting earnestly with Frank Pate when Wayne Holland came in. He took what was quickly becoming his regular seat at the counter and nodded to Eloise.

"Breakfast, dinner, or lunch?" I asked him.

He looked confused. "It's Friday, right? In the afternoon?"

"Ye-es," I said cautiously.

"I lose track on graveyard shift. Once I got up and went out for breakfast. Turned out to be six-thirty in the evening." He took the menu I held out and stared at it for a minute. "I'd better have coffee."

I thought he'd better have coffee, too, so I poured a cup from the older, stronger pot and set it in front of him.

Wayne closed the menu and looked at me with big, grateful eyes. I almost fell for it. Until I remembered that I'd sworn off men.

"Take your time," I told him. "I'll be here when you're ready." Then realizing how loosely that might be interpreted, I added, "To order."

Eloise had finished her cigarette and patted her already perfect hair. I saw her coming, with a gleam in her eye, and hurried to the other end of the counter to stack cups. To my great surprise and relief, she appeared not to notice me.

Leaning casually on the counter, she smiled sympathetically at Wayne. "Shift work. You'd think it'd get easier after a while."

"Yeah, but it never does." Wayne's voice was still cramped by sleep and sounded as if it had come all the way up from his toenails.

"My third husband worked swing shift. He was

a terror on graveyards." Eloise gave a little
chuckle. "Course, he claimed I got bitchy when he
worked nights. Said I went out of my way to irri-
tate him."

Wayne nodded as if he understood. "I might as
well eat," he said. "Can I get a hot brown here?"

"Shoot, yeah. Matter of fact, I'll have one with
you. It's almost dinnertime." Eloise checked her
watch, wrote an order on her pad, and ducked into
the kitchen to hand it to the cook. She was back in
ten seconds.

All this had piqued my curiosity. There I was,
trapped behind the counter, and Eloise hadn't made
any attempt to throw me at Wayne. I took the tray
that had held clean cups back to the kitchen and,
while there, surreptitiously checked the dinner order Eloise had written to be sure it didn't include
a note telling the cook to throw in a handful of love
dust. This doesn't necessarily mean I'm paranoid.

The bell on the front door jingled just as I'd assured myself that Eloise was giving Wayne a genuine hot brown. Peeking through the serving
window, I saw that Benny and Chester had finished
their dinner. I know their routine so well, I didn't
even have to ask. I served up lemon ice-box pie for
both, skimming the meringue off Benny's. (Actually, his request is, "Peel off the calf slobber.") I
made a round with the coffeepot, cleared a table,
pocketed the tip, and returned to the counter. Eloise
was still chatting at Wayne.

Wayne seemed to be perking up, as men do
around Eloise, so I felt it was time to refill his cup
with decent coffee. Eloise glanced up at me and
smiled like a proud mother. "Kay, honey, would
you pour me a cup of that? I need a little caffeine
about this time of day."

"Sure," I said, waiting a beat for her to make a

pitch. She didn't—just turned back to Wayne and asked about his position at Land. While fixing Eloise coffee and arranging setups for both of them, I learned that Wayne Holland had been employed by Land for fifteen years, was a backtender (he did not explain what a backtender does), and knew at least one of Eloise's ex-husbands.

And then their order came up, followed by a couple more customers just as I was delivering tabs to Benny and Chester. First one thing then another kept me moderately busy, and by the time I settled down, it was the end of my shift.

"Head on home," Eloise told me. "I've got it until Jenny gets here." Jenny being the high school girl who works evenings and weekends.

"I can stick around," I offered while grabbing my purse and jacket from under the counter. Outside the clouds were thick and looked as if they were about ten feet off the ground. Just as I straightened up, the deluge began. Rain was pounding down so hard I could barely see the courthouse across the street.

"Oh, dear," Eloise said as the sign out front started swinging, "this looks like it'll go on for a while. You'll drown if you try to walk home."

There was a brief silence, and then Wayne said, "I can give you a lift."

There was a longer silence while I processed the offer. "I'd appreciate that," I said finally.

After he'd paid for his meal, Wayne and I made a mad dash for the red pickup truck parked directly in front of the diner. This took a mere eight seconds, but we were both drenched by the time I slammed my door.

"Cloth seats! They'll be ruined." I felt genuinely guilty. It was obvious that Wayne was one of those men who valued his truck above all else. The dash and floor were spotless, and even the wood trim had been recently cleaned with lemon-scented furniture polish.

"It'll dry," he said, but there was a note of grief in his voice.

While Wayne fumbled for keys and adjusted lights, wipers, and defogger, I leaned over to check the tape in his cassette player. You can tell a lot about a man from his music.

"Nanci Griffith? Is this yours?"

Wayne nodded and eased the truck onto the street.

"You like Nanci Griffith?"

"I like a lot of things," he said defensively. "Rod Stewart, Hank Williams."

"You're kidding."

"Senior," he added. He pulled the truck over to the curb in front of my house and turned to face me. "Call me moody. Or fickle. Or plain unde- cided."

"It's just odd," I said. "Most people like country or rock or jazz or classical."

"I don't have any Beethoven," he said, and smiled. Dimples hiding under his beard suddenly popped out. "I'm too down-home for that."

"Well, thanks for the ride." I pulled my jacket over my head, tucked my purse under one arm, and reached for the door handle. "I'm sorry about the wet seat—wait a minute. How did you know this was my house?"

"I know all sorts of things." Deadpan.

I gave him a determined stare, but he just sat there looking pleasant and friendly; so I opened the door and shouted, "Thanks again," as I jumped out. I slammed the door shut and ran like crazy up the walk and into the covered porch.

For a few minutes I just stood there pretending

to shake water off my jacket and watching Wayne Holland's truck pull away. In the pouring rain I couldn't get a clear view of Primrose Lane, the one-way street that stretches north and runs parallel to Morning Glory, but I was sure I caught a glimpse of red taillights as Wayne headed back to the main highway. I could imagine him driving through the gloomy afternoon and singing along with Nanci or Rod or Hank. I was so taken with that image that I barely noticed the mutilated door when I went inside.

I did, however, notice that Wayne Holland was starting to grow on me. In keeping with my policy of expending the least possible energy, I've avoided logic whenever possible. I work on intuition. And while my brain told me caution was in order, my soul purred like Bella on a sunny afternoon.

CHAPTER
14

Death: The old order is ended; a new phase begins.

THE HOUSE WAS EMPTY, FULL OF DAMP
and gloom from the storm outside. I went through,
turning on lights and electric heaters and mum-
bling, "Damn the electric bill," as I went.

John wanders about at will, adhering to no one's
schedule, so I wasn't surprised to find the house
empty. And maybe it was just the end of a long day,
or the miserable weather or the relentless boredom
that got to me, but for a change, I would have
begged him to sit in the frayed chair and rip into
my psyche.

While the tub filled with hot water, I gathered a
flannel gown and a pair of socks, stripped in the
bathroom and stuffed my grease-stained uniform
into the hamper, and poured a half bottle of Lady
Mystique Beauty Bath into the water. Then I
crawled in and let my body slide until my chin was
under the bubbles and I could inhale the steam rising up.

I didn't know how on edge I was until the phone rang and I jumped half out of the water. The cold air may have been responsible for the goose bumps on my arms, but the chill that ran down my spine was a direct result of *Psycho* memories.

I wrapped the nearest towel around me and padded into the living room. It took only three rings for me to accomplish this, but the jangling had really frayed my nerves. When I snatched up the receiver, I practically growled.

"Hey!" said the friendly, unintimidated voice of Wayne Holland.

"Hey," I answered back.

"I'm just checking to make sure you got home okay."

I went blank for a minute, convinced that I'd imagined the ride home. "Weren't you just here?" I asked.

"I mean, did you get inside and everything?"

Did I get inside? What a question! You can understand why it took me a minute to figure out that he'd probably just heard about the incident of the night before. I wasn't sure whether to be touched or worried.

"Yes," I said at last. "No problems."

"Well, look," he said, with great confidence, "would you like to do something after work tomorrow?"

"Like what?" No, I was not being coy. It had been a century since anyone had asked me out.

"Like take a ride or have dinner. Can't go to a movie because I work tomorrow night, but . . ."

Any other time I would have stuck to my guns and forced myself to dislike Wayne Holland on general principle. But I suppose I was vunerable at that moment. I *had* promised myself I'd put some zest in my life. And I wasn't a bit happy about the cozy way I'd been feeling toward John. Clearly what I needed was a social life, even if it came to nothing more than riding around in Wayne's truck and listening to his tape collection.

I gave in to intuition and decided to trust him.

After Wayne's phone call, I dressed in my familiar flannel gown and fixed a bologna sandwich, promising myself that I'd buy hot dogs on my next trip to the store. Bologna is bologna. You just can't disguise it. And frankly, I was sick of cold-cut cuisine. I was equally sick of watching the same old TV programs, but there wasn't much I could do about that.

Friday night has its own special personality. There's the feeling of electricity, like the night before a favorite holiday. I suppose that's why my great depressions so often occur around ten on Friday night—because I know Saturday will be a tremendous letdown, no matter what nebulous thrill I may have expected. I began to have doubts about going out with Wayne while I pondered this and other dismal truths, but decided it would serve me right to be miserable. That would teach me to give in to my codependent urges, wouldn't it?

I'd loaded the coffee table with chips, dip, cookies, and a family-size bag of peanut M&M's. In my lap I had a yellow legal pad and my favorite writing pen. Every time I completed a line of my new poem (working title: "Saturday Afternoon among Shadows"), I'd reward myself with a snack. Simple pleasures.

Halfway through the poem, which wasn't progressing to my satisfaction, I decided to type up a few of my finished poems and get them ready to mail. When I entered John's abnormally tidy room to get the typewriter, I noticed a stack of ungraded math papers on his bed. Unlike him to leave that task undone, I thought. He's usually right on top of his work. Whatever he was up to must have been important.

Back in the living room, I readied nine poems for the next day's mail. I'm a reasonably fast typist, but I kept stopping for snacks. I also stopped every time a branch scratched against the house or the thunder rolled over with the force of a kamikaze attack. I did not feel that I was especially jittery, though. Seems to me any woman who's just had satanic threats left on her doorstep ought to be aware of what's going on around her.

Added to this was the infuriating news tease. The promos kept promising "a disturbing new development in the Night Terror case. Details at ten." I don't think I'm a callous person, but frankly I was getting sick of this media obsession. Didn't robberies still occur? Hadn't a dictator been toppled lately? Or had the Night Terror so captured the world's attention that everyone had decided to stay home and out of trouble until he was caught?

I was out of dip, and I'd decided to finish the potato chips by eating them alternately with bites of white chocolate I'd found stashed under the *TV Guide*. I was estimating a three-pound weight gain for the evening when I heard John's car pull up out front.

"You've eaten everything in the house," he wailed when he saw the ruins on the coffee table. He stood there dripping on the shag.

"There's bologna left," I told him. "And a few cookies. You're welcome to those. I couldn't eat another bite."

"I'm sure," John said. "Would you excuse me a minute while I change?" He started toward his bedroom.

"I borrowed your typewriter," I called after him. "I'll put it back when you're through."

John stopped in the hallway, as if he hadn't heard me clearly, then said, "No problem. Did you happen to grade those test papers while you were at it?"

"Fat chance," I called absently. I was waiting for him to emerge in dry clothing before I told him about my date. The thought of telling him about it bothered me. After the trouble he'd given me over the King of Cups, I was sure I'd never hear the end of this. Sometimes it seemed as if John was more concerned about my personal life than about his own. But perhaps, I thought, he'll behave like an adult just this once and keep his mouth shut.

Needless to say, that was a ridiculous hope. "A date?" He smirked. "A *date*?"

"Well . . . not exactly a date."

"Of course it's a date. The cards told you he'd be coming along, didn't they? Or rather, I told you, since cards have to be interpreted. Just leave a necktie on the doorknob."

John had made his own bologna sandwich and was devouring it at the coffee table while I nibbled on the potato chip crumbs.

"I'll say this once, John. I don't want to be bugged about going out with Wayne. It's not as if I'm smitten with him, or even interested in pursuing a relationship. But I'm tired of sitting around the house all the time."

"Well, if that's all it is, I could take you out."

"It's not the same thing," I pointed out.

"It could be."

Well, yes. It could have been, which is exactly why I would never go out with John. In fact, I wouldn't even tell him that much because he's so easily encouraged.

"The news will be on in a minute. They claim there's some development on the Night Terror. Want to watch?"

John didn't answer, but he held his sandwich in one hand and grabbed his coffee cup with the other, while burrowing comfortably into his chair. We were both fighting for the last potato chip when the program began.

"Another letter from the Night Terror," the anchorman said ominously. "This one contains gruesome proof of the writer's identity."

I was spellbound. Nothing could have pried me away from that television, not even the string of endless commercials that were forced upon me while I waited for details.

"You don't think he sent one of the fingers?" I asked John.

"Wouldn't think so," he said nonchalantly. "I expect he's had all those bronzed."

The anchor, when he returned, finally got to the heart of the story. The Night Terror's letter was flashed on the screen. It was a scrawled mess, but the anchor translated for us.

"The letter was received this morning by Angela County Law enforcement officials," he explained.

"Reb didn't mention that! Darn him!" I could have clobbered the man.

John shushed me as the anchor continued.

"The letter reads: 'You are not the center of the universe, but you are the center of my universe. Now that you have found my first offering, I leave you to guess where I will appear next. Your next move should be to follow the sun.'"

The anchorman then explained that Nita's body had been found in Angela County and that experts had concluded that her death had occurred before any of the others.

"Included with the letter," he went on, "was a scrap of fabric, determined to have come from the clothing worn by Nita Lowry when she was killed."

"Cocky, isn't he?" I said to John. Even I was starting to get immune to the Night Terror's behavior. "Do you suppose he's ready to be caught?"

"You've been talking to Clara Maddox again, haven't you? If he wanted to get caught, he'd turn himself in."

"Oh, John. They always want to get caught. Can you think of any other reason he'd write a letter and even give the police a clue about his next move?"

John nodded. "Sure. He knows he's smarter than they are and he's playing games with them. It's a power trip for him. Some people are so intelligent they get bored dealing with puny minds. They have to make up their own forms of entertainment."

"Like you?" I smiled sweetly at him. "I could use the reward money, so if you're the killer, please say so now. I'll turn you in."

"Ha! You wouldn't have the heart." John was smug. He knows I'm a sucker for lost causes.

Despite my happy-go-lucky attitude in the evening, by the time I crawled into bed I was anxious again. The police were not sufficiently motivated, I decided. After all, it wasn't cops who were being stalked and murdered by a deranged digit collector.

Perhaps I wasn't in real danger either. John could have been right—my door might have been defaced by an aspiring artist who couldn't get his work shown anywhere else. Certainly there'd been times when I'd considered hiring a skywriter to get my poems into public view.

But whether the Night Terror had left that note for me, or whether it had been a malicious prank,

I wanted the matter resolved. Reb had promised to check around town and find out if anyone else had received the same surprise. The fact that he hadn't gotten back to me probably meant I was the only victim, and that made it even more likely to be a serious threat.

It had not escaped my attention, either, that the next day—Saturday—would be the tenth day since the last of the Night Terror attacks. If he stayed with the schedule, someone would be murdered within the next twenty-four hours.

CHAPTER

15

Temperance: Know when to pursue and when to retreat.

WAYNE PICKED ME UP AT FIVE, KNOCKING
on the front door like a perfect gentleman. John,
needless to say, had found reason to hang around
the house, and he bounded to his feet to introduce
himself.

The two men danced graciously around each other,
Wayne obviously reluctant to ask about my male
roommate, and John trying to play the father role.

"Not much to do around Jesus Creek," he pointed
out. "I guess you two will have to look elsewhere
for entertainment."

Wayne, still standing in the middle of the living
room while I burrowed through the closet for a
jacket, just nodded. "You're right about Jesus
Creek. I guess Kay and I will have to talk it over.
I thought about having dinner, but Eloise's is the
best place in town and I didn't figure Kay would
want to be there again after she's worked all day."

"Darned right!" I agreed. "But we'll think of something." Having found a sweatshirt and my purse, I was all set. "But I dressed for Jesus Creek," I said, "so don't insist on anything fancy."

Since Wayne was dressed almost exactly as I was, I felt safe. Ordinarily I'd have worked harder on my appearance, but I was striving to avoid the idea of *date*. I didn't think jeans constituted anything more than an outing with a new acquaintance.

John saw us to the door, his arm protectively around my shoulders. "Good to meet you," he said to Wayne as we stepped onto the porch. "Kay's told me a lot about you."

I turned slightly to release myself from John's arm, making a discreet but meaningful face at him as I did so.

Wayne and I drove off in his newly cleaned truck and got as far as the park before he pulled to the side of the road and stopped.

"Have you seen the statue?" he asked.

"No. Have you?"

"I wouldn't dare," he said quickly. "Roger is serious about this. He gave me a five-minute lecture on the importance of keeping peekers away. Then he made me raise my right hand and swear to protect the secret of the statue with my life."

"Yes, that sounds like Roger. I see Benny and Chester are on duty today." The two little old men were standing on either side of the covered statue in poses that would have earned them honorary membership in the Coldstream Guard.

Grass was just beginning to turn green in the park, and the new maples were sprouting first growth. The sun was still out but was low enough in the western sky to cast intriguing shadows across the ground. Here and there were carefully shaped beds, where the Sons and Daughters of the Confederacy had planted flowers. Once upon a time we'd had a bench in the park, but that had been lost in an accident the year before. Not that anyone had ever used it anyway.

"Would you like to stop and get a closer look?" Wayne asked.

I shook my head. "Benny and Chester might whop us with those sticks. But food sounds fine. Can you think of anyplace other than Eloise's that would let us in?"

Wayne started up the truck again and pushed in the Nanci Griffith tape. "Maybe we can just pick up sandwiches somewhere and take them with us."

"You have to go to work tonight, right?" I asked. "I don't want to drag you off too far. I guess you need to nap a bit before you go in."

"No problem," Wayne said. "It's tomorrow that worries me—I've promised to guard the statue after I get off in the morning."

"Shouldn't be too much work. Everybody else will be in church, and you won't have to worry about them trying to crawl under the tarp."

We drove on toward the river, stopping only at a bait shop to pick up ham sandwiches and drinks. Wayne seemed to be making an effort to talk, at least. I'd worried that we might spend the evening in silence. But he seemed positively fascinated when I mentioned my poetry.

"I don't know how you can think of anything to write," he confessed. "I had one teacher in high school who was always trying to get us to appreciate poetry. Don't think anybody ever did."

"Well, I didn't care for it in school, either," I admitted. "But I'll show you some of mine sometime. It usually makes more sense than the stuff in textbooks." I'd found a new project—teaching Wayne

Holland to appreciate fine literature. Starting with my poetry.

Just before we crossed the bridge that would have taken us into Benton Harbor, Wayne turned north onto a rutted dirt road. "Have you ever been out this way?" he asked.

"Not on purpose. Why?" You're right if you think I was starting to get nervous about wandering off into the boonies with this man. But I didn't want to jump from the truck, screaming and yelling. No pun intended, but I'd rather die than make a fool of myself.

"If you follow this road far enough, you wind up in Plant. That's where Jesse James used to live."

"Really? I thought it was closer to the county line."

"He lived right here in Plant. Tried farming, I think. I'm not sure exactly where the house was, but I ran into a lady from the community the other day and she gave me directions. How long have you lived in Jesus Creek, anyway?"

"All my life," I said. "Nobody gets out of this town."

"And you've never visited the Jesse James home?" He hit one of the larger ruts and we bounced around the cab a couple of times.

"No, but then history isn't my favorite subject. It's so damned hard to talk about anything else in this town, I guess I just got sick of it."

"You're right about that. Everybody's hung up on their ancestors. Funny they're not like that in Benton Harbor. You'd think, the towns being so close together—"

"Well, that much history I do understand. When Jesus Creek was first founded, the settlers kept pretty much to themselves. I don't think they really liked visitors from the other communities. And the tradition continues. It's almost like we've been cut off from the world all along. I know people who've lived in Jesus Creek for over thirty years, but they're still considered outsiders."

"Gosh, I'm surprised they let me move in at all." Wayne steered the truck deftly along the road as it got narrower and curvier.

We were heading into uncharted territory, as far as I was concerned. When a road becomes too narrow for a standard vehicle to travel without brushing the trees on either side, I quit. But Wayne didn't seem to be bothered by it, although he did grimace every time one of the branches screeched across the customized paint job on his precious truck.

"Are you sure you know where you're going?" I asked. Don't think I didn't have my purse clutched tightly to my chest, just in case I had to defend myself. But I was feeling more and more secure as I rode along with Wayne. No doubt Kate Yancy's psychic would have said he had a trustworthy aura. I couldn't see his aura, but my own receptors were satisfied that he could be trusted.

"Fairly sure," he said. "This road should come out onto a blacktop, right near the James place."

"Do they still call it that?"

"No. It belongs to a local family." Wayne gritted his teeth as another low-growing tree limb brushed us on the passenger side.

And then the road opened up, and ahead of us I could see that the dirt trail led to the paved road Wayne had mentioned. Even after we made the turn, it still seemed like boonies to me.

"This is it," Wayne said, turning into a rutted wide spot on the side of the road.

We'd parked in front of a small garage. Behind it, and off to the right, stood a house that had obviously been built recently, but designed with the spirit of history in mind.

"I don't suppose that's where Jesse lived?" I said doubtfully.

"The house Jesse lived in is gone now," Wayne told me. He opened the driver's side door and stepped out, then held out his hand to me. "Come on. We're going through the pasture." He clearly meant the fenced area to the left of the garage.

I slid across the seat and let him help me out of the truck, my purse still protectively at my side. "Do you think we should be trespassing like this? Usually when folks put up an electric fence they mean for strangers to stay on the outside of it."

"Don't worry. They'll shoot us if they don't want us here." Wayne threw first one leg then the other over the low wire fence and turned to help me across. Then he pointed with assurance to a tree growing down the gently sloping hillside. "There it is."

I looked dutifully but couldn't imagine what on earth he thought he'd found. "Is that where the house sat or something?"

"It's the graves," he said.

"Jesse James is buried here?" I couldn't believe I'd missed that bit of history.

Wayne started walking through the field while I struggled to keep up with him. I had not had the foresight, as Wayne had, to wear boots, so I had to pick my way carefully around the cow patties.

"No, not Jesse. His sons. They were just babies when they died. Twins."

We finally stopped beside a small grave marker that bore the names of Jesse's twin sons: Montgomery and Gould. "This marker was put up a few years ago," Wayne explained. "I'm not sure where the original is, but I expect it's here in the pasture somewhere. You want to look for it?"

"Not really," I said, attempting to scrape the bottom of my shoe clean. "Hard to imagine Jesse James having children, isn't it? When I think of outlaws, I get a completely different picture."

Wayne nodded. "I suppose they're like everybody else, though. Just regular folks once they get home from work."

"Even if work involves slaughtering dozens of people for the fun of it?"

"Well, Jesse tried his best. He moved here to be a farmer, after all. According to the stories, he was pretty much the gentleman. They even called him the Rabbit Man around here, because he wouldn't fight back when anybody challenged him."

"Rabbit Man? I don't know, Wayne. I think Jesse had it in him to kill and there was no way to make him change."

Wayne didn't answer right away, and when he did I wasn't sure I understood the connection. "I wonder," he said, "why there's no monument."

I firmly vetoed Wayne's idea about eating our dinner there by the children's grave, so we drove back over the dirt road to Jesus Creek and down to the river. Along the way Wayne pointed out houses and cemeteries of interest to anyone excited by local history. I couldn't imagine how he'd come to know the area so well in so short a time.

"The lady who told me about the James place gave me a quick tour. There's a lot of history here. I'll bet she'd take you around, too, if you asked her."

I promised to consider it. Funny, I thought, how Wayne is already fitting into the Jesus Creek state of mind.

When we got to the river, the sun was just dip-

ping into the water, backlighting the trees along
the opposite shore. There's no real boat dock in
Jesus Creek, just one section of riverbank that
slopes into the water. Someone had thoughtfully
placed a wooden picnic table there for travelers such
as Wayne and myself, so we took advantage of it
and spread ourselves out to relax.

The weather was perfect for picnicking, too. A
slight breeze kept the water lapping the shore. The
temperature had climbed to the mid-seventies earlier in the day and held steady there even as dusk
took hold. We ate with our backs to the highway
and watched the sun slowly disappear.

By the time we'd finished our sandwiches and
carefully disposed of our wrappers in Wayne's litter
bag, I was feeling like a woman who'd just been
cured of a dreadful disease.

"Have you been to the Knob?" Wayne asked.
He'd moved around to my side of the table and was
sitting next to me. Close enough to be friendly, but
not so close that I worried.

"A long time ago," I answered. The Knob is
downriver from Jesus Creek, technically outside our
area of legitimate historical interest. On the Benton Harbor side, it's a hill that juts above the others just enough to be noticed. I remembered that
some battle of the Civil War had been fought there.

"Are you a battle buff?" I asked Wayne.

"Naw," he said. "I just pick things up here and
there."

I was getting drowsy, and I thought he must be,
too. After all, he'd been up all night. So to be nice,
I asked if he'd like to call it a day.

"I hate to admit it," he said, "but I'm pretty tired.
It must be old age or something. I remember one
time I stayed up for seventy-two hours straight. Of

course, that's when I was dating my ex-wife, and I did a lot of stupid things back then."

To give you an idea of just how mellow I was by then, I mentally cursed his ex for not taking better care of him.

"Let's take you home," I said briskly, and stood up. Reaching for his hand, I pulled Wayne to his feet. "If you'd like, I'll drive. You can nap on the way."

For an instant, I saw pure terror flicker across his face as he considered the idea of my driving his precious truck. Then, like a knight about to enter the dragon's cave, he said, "Okay. You can drive."

Wayne had deposited me at my door without so much as a handshake. I was relieved and yet mildly offended. As I kicked off my shoes and disposed of my sweatshirt and purse, I realized with great surprise that I'd had fun. It had been a mild, quiet, pleasant date. Outing, rather.

John was closed up in his room, but I heard the clacking of his typewriter. I'd offered to teach him to use more than two fingers, but John is a stubborn man.

I knocked gently on the door and heard a chair scrape across the hardwood floor. In two seconds he flung open the door and adopted a fatherly tone to demand, "Young lady, do you know what time it is?"

"Get off it. I didn't mean to interrupt. Just thought you'd want to know I'm still alive."

John stepped out into the hall and pulled the bedroom door closed. "But is your heart still your own?"

"I'll make coffee if you'll promise not to make a big deal of this date." I led the way to the kitchen, while John snickered quietly behind me.

"Wayne is charming," I said, while I filled the pot with water. "We went out to Jesse James's place. Ate sandwiches by the river. That's about it."

"I didn't ask."

"But you would have eventually. Have you eaten?"

He nodded. "Several times. Sarah Elizabeth dropped by while you were gone. Otherwise I've been sitting alone and unloved in my empty room."

I've learned that John's facetiousness is a cover. He pretends to be self-sufficient, but he really is a lonely man. Sometimes I want to grab him and hug him and make him understand that we all adore his irritating ways. But he'd hate that. John cherishes his facade of invulnerability.

With coffee brewing and John once again raiding the fridge, I sat down at the table and propped my feet up in one of the other chairs. "What sort of deviousness were you up to just now? With the typewriter?"

"Application," John said around a mouthful of cheese. "Thought I'd try to make the summer semester at APSU."

"You're going back to school? I didn't know you'd been thinking about that."

John dropped an armful of sandwich makings on the counter and began to assemble the most god-awful snack I've ever seen. Mayonnaise *and* catsup! "I decided it's about time I got back to it. Either finish the degree or teach at JCHS for the rest of my miserable life."

It pleased me to learn that John had plans. He was far too intelligent to content himself with odd teaching jobs in a small town. On the other hand, if he got a real job somewhere else, I'd be out a roommate. And I'd grown quite comfortable with John's company.

"Will you be driving back and forth to school, or . . . ?"

"Yeah. For a while. Why don't you apply, too?"

"Because I can't afford it."

"Too bad you're not a recovering alcoholic. Or a recovering veteran."

Since John was both, he seldom had to worry about how to pay his educational expenses. He'd managed to discover government grants to cover almost any occasion.

"Even with the money," I went on, "what would I do? I haven't the slightest idea what I want to be when I grow up."

"It doesn't matter what you do, as long as you continue forward."

"Straight on till morning, right?"

"I didn't say straight," John pointed out. "I said continue forward. There's a big difference."

"Really? What is it?"

John smiled tolerantly and arched his eyebrows. "Think about it."

We carried coffee and John's sandwich into the living room and made ourselves comfortable in front of the tube.

"News?" John asked, flipping on the set. "Or a sitcom?"

"The news, I guess. Might as well find out what stupid and depressing things have happened in the world lately."

We waited through two commercials for the anchorman, who, with appropriate solemnity, informed us that another victim of the Night Terror had been discovered just moments earlier.

CHAPTER
16

The Devil: Fear is crippling; do not let the cloud of illusion blind you to truth.

TO BE ACCURATE, A BODY HAD BEEN FOUND and the Night Terror was suspected. While we waited through the theme music and opening credits, I felt my stomach clenching with the absolute certainty that the Night Terror had struck again. The only question I had was, had Jesus Creek once again been targeted?

"Moments ago," the anchorman began, "the body of a woman was found at a roadside park in Benton Harbor, just west of the Tennessee River."

I felt my stomach roll over.

"Authorities working on the case have refused to comment on the latest killing, except to say that they are not yet able to confirm or deny rumors that this is another in a series of deaths attributed to the Night Terror."

I looked at John to see what he thought of the

situation. He was happily finishing his meal, but listening intently to the story.

"It's the Night Terror," I said firmly.

"Could be."

"But not in Jesus Creek. Why did he start here and then move east?"

John put his empty plate down on the coffee table and leaned back in his chair. "May not make sense to anyone but him. You have to admire his cunning, don't you?"

"I don't admire anything about him."

"You've been reading up on serial killers, right? Aren't they all described as average men, going about their business just like always?"

I flashed on the Rabbit Man, suddenly enlightened.

"Of course, that's the problem. Being average isn't respectable. Serial killers are trying to build their own self-esteem, taking lives like hunters mount trophies. It's a sign of manhood."

"My, you have been giving this a lot of thought."

I ignored John's gibe and continued to muse aloud. "But why do they keep souvenirs? That's not something they'd want to show to friends. What's the point?"

John shrugged, as if the answer should have been obvious. "The killer himself can have a grand old time reliving the experience through his collection. And then there's the man—or woman—who kills to regain power over his or her own life. Haven't you ever felt out of control, as if the universe is bouncing you around?"

"Yes," I admitted, "but I've never considered killing someone to make it better."

"You never considered killing Gary?" John raised his eyebrow and waited.

"Not seriously." Okay, so I lied a little.

John stood up and stretched his arms over his head, then yawned. He picked up his plate and cup and started for the kitchen. "I counseled inmates at Bald Knob," he reminded me. "Some of them were pretty interesting men. Told me a lot of things they'd never admit to anybody else. One of them claimed to have been asleep when he robbed that bank. Nonsense, of course. But a good con is like a good magician—he uses misdirection to make you believe anything."

The anchorman promised details as they became available. I sneered but made plans to stay by the television for a while. In the meantime, I called Clara Maddox to remind her that she was hosting a Lady Mystique event on Monday night. People do forget, believe it or not, and part of my job is to be sure they've invited their guests.

"I just wonder," Clara said, "if it's wise to encourage women to be out after dark."

I could feel sales slipping away, so I quickly assured her. "Don't worry about that, Clara. We'll be in a group, after all. That should keep us safe. And we certainly don't want to let this lunatic hold us prisoners in our own homes, do we?" I knew appealing to her rebellious nature would work.

"No doubt you're right," she said, sounding determined. "Then I'll see you at six?"

Relieved, I went on to explain that I'd be doing her free makeover, that refreshments should consist of simple fare, and I asked her to set up her card table beforehand. If anyone ever reports that to the Lady Mystique company, I'll probably get fired.

"I guess you've heard," she said then, "that they've found another victim."

"Yes. Just now on the news."

"Well, Devereux was talking to his friend tonight. You know, the TBI agent I've mentioned. This latest one has them all so confused they don't know which end is up."

I wasn't sure that Clara knew what she was talking about, but I couldn't very well pass up an opportunity like that, could I? "Really?" I said nonchalantly. "How so?"

"Well, for one thing, they found the body in Benton Harbor. You know, they've been running every which way since Nita Lowry was found, because that just didn't seem to fit any pattern at all."

"John thinks the killer has a pattern that no one's identified yet."

Clara agreed. "I'm sure that's so. But we can't expect our policemen to follow *that* train of thought, can we? After all, the Night Terror is obviously insane. What makes sense to him would be incomprehensible to normal people." Clara paused a second for breath, then went on. "There's one more thing, too. The victim they found today isn't exactly blonde."

"A killer wouldn't necessarily take time to check the roots, Clara," I pointed out. Then feeling that I ought to promote the product, I added, "And *some* hair color, such as Lady Mystique, looks so natural—"

"For heaven's sake, Kay. I mean the girl was black. African-American, that is."

That gave me a shake, but it quickly became obvious that we'd all jumped to conclusions. "Then it's not the Night Terror," I said, with great conviction. "Just one of those copycat killers. Don't you think?"

"I shouldn't be saying this. Devereux will just kill me if he finds out. But just between you and me, Kay—this one's worse. I can't say any more than that."

Try as I might, I couldn't convince her to spill any more of what she knew. Of course, she'd probably exaggerated the whole business anyway. By the time we hung up, I was not only frustrated, but fed up. Anyone who listens to Clara's nonsense, I reminded myself, deserves to be irritated by it.

John had tidied the kitchen and retreated to his room. The next day, Sunday, was my second day off. I'd have given anything to get two days off in a row, but Eloise simply hadn't been able to schedule it that way. Good help is hard to find, and Jenny had both dance class and voice lessons on Saturday.

But because Sunday was my free day, I decided to make the most of Saturday evening. It really was too bad, I decided, that Wayne had to work that night. We might have enjoyed going all out for a movie and a hot dog. Lacking companionship of any kind, I dug out the notes I'd made on serial killers and the books I'd checked out of the library.

One section claimed that killers who leave their victims in the open *want* them to be found and given a decent burial. This suggests that the killer has some compassion. I found that hard to believe. Compassionate souls do not, as a rule, torture, rape, murder, and mutilate other human beings.

I wondered about Clara's comment that "this one had been worse." Sometimes a brutal attack indicates a close relationship between the killer and victim. (I paused here to consider what Gary's body might have looked like if I'd ever given in to my killer instinct.) Maybe the woman they'd found in Benton Harbor was another victim of domestic abuse, rather than of the Night Terror. Still, the timing was right. Ten days.

Suddenly it occurred to me that there might be a clue in that. Jack the Ripper's victims were most often killed on weekends, which might have meant that Jack was wandering into London for holiday at the end of the week. Why was the Night Terror so stuck on this ten day bit?

I was more than a little grateful for the work schedule at the Land plant. The shifts there change every seven days; had it been ten, I'd have been more likely to fall for John's insinuation that Wayne was responsible.

As I turned page after page in the books I'd borrowed, I found enough information to make me dizzy. Unfortunately, most of it could have applied to anyone. Many serial killers, I learned, come from single-parent homes and have difficulty relating to women. It's the Nineties, folks. Divorce is rampant. And from my experiences with men, I'd say they *all* have trouble relating.

I cocked an ear toward John's bedroom door. The profiles fit *him* as well as anybody. Was it possible that he'd been slipping out the window at night and stalking women? I was relieved to hear the clumsy tapping of the typewriter that reassured me he was really in there working. Unless he'd merely tape-recorded himself typing and—

Was I losing it? Clearly I'd been watching too much television and dwelling *way* too much on the serial-killer profile. Okay, back to the books.

CHAPTER
17

The Tower, reversed: The walls are destroyed and the old ways ended forever.

SUNDAY MORNING WAS A MASTERPIECE. The temperature had reached the seventies by the time I woke up. A gentle breeze had the trees nodding like good little children minding their mothers. And through the kitchen window I could see blackbirds pecking around for treats. Call me easy. That's all it took to put me in a cheerful mood.

John had already made coffee, but he was cloistered in his bedroom. I could hear the typewriter clicking. For the sake of his index fingers, I hoped he didn't have many more applications to fill out.

Feeling that a morning so perfect shouldn't be wasted, I dressed quickly in jeans and a T-shirt and set out to enjoy the beauty that was Jesus Creek. Heading south on Morning Glory, I passed a row of houses that looked similar to mine. Except, of course, that mine had the screened front porch whereas the others were fronted merely by little

square, roofed concrete blocks. The grass wasn't
green, nor had the trees yet displayed their color,
but bright sunshine and a warm breeze were trade-
offs.

The third house down from mine is Delia Cannon's, and she was already outside, basking in the
morning. Roger was nowhere in sight. Delia is good
about keeping her house painted and her lawn
trimmed, and she tries hard to nourish and encourage the row of tulips that grow along the walk to
the porch. Unfortunately, her thumb only turns
green when she's around that tangled mass of
weeds in the backyard that she calls an herb garden.

"Lost the Yankee, have you?" I asked as I headed
up the path to her front porch. Poor Roger takes a
lot of ribbing from the history buffs about his family's position during the Civil War.

"He's installing new members into the militia,"
she said. Meaning, of course, that he was checking
on the statue. "Your friend Wayne is on duty this
morning, isn't he?"

"*My* friend?" I said as I joined her on the porch.

"As far as I know, you're the only one in town
who's dated him." Delia smiled slyly. The local
grapevine was still in operation.

"It wasn't a date. Just an outing, thank you."

"So you aren't going out with him again?"

I thought about it for a minute, then answered
honestly. "He hasn't asked me."

"You could ask him, you know."

"I could. But that sort of obligates me, doesn't it?
I'm not sure I want to see him again."

"So if he does ask, you'll say no."

"For pity's sake, Delia, must I decide right this
minute?"

Delia let the topic pass, knowing full well that I

probably wouldn't turn him down. "Have you seen the parade lineup?"

"Not yet. Is it posted at the hardware store?"

Delia nodded. "They've got Glenda on the lead float. They probably *think* she'll be wearing green tights and a micromini. I rather suspect Frank Pate and the other organizers will be disappointed."

"Got the usual bunch? Shriners, clowns, high school band?"

"Uhm-hmm. Plus Mary Anne's basset hound, no doubt wearing a shamrock wreath around his neck. And the nursing home float, of course."

I was glad to hear the nursing home would be participating. The residents there seem to put more effort into their parade entries than most other folks. The mobile elderly climb aboard the float and toss candy to bystanders. Others are pushed along the parade route in their wheelchairs. I told you, *all* of Jesus Creek gets involved in this celebration.

"I hope the Night Terror doesn't spoil the parade," I said absently, thinking how unreal the killer seemed on this peaceful day.

"I suppose you've heard abut the body they found across the river."

I nodded, and for a few seconds we both stared up at the bright blue of the sky, covered here and there by innocent clouds. Fire is a purifying element, and sunlight is the next best thing. I wondered if we'd been given this glorious day to vanquish the gloom that had been hounding us for weeks now. At that moment, it seemed as if it might work.

"I'm going to Nita's funeral on Tuesday," Delia said. "What a sweet girl. I always hated that she married that man, though."

"The funeral will be tough on Reb, too. Did she have a big family?"

Delia shook her head. "I gather her father died

several years ago. Of course, she was originally from Benton Harbor, so I don't know her family."

"It's almost impossible to believe—that a tragedy like this could happen here in Jesus Creek."

"A year ago I'd have agreed. Lately I've come to expect it every time I open the door."

Delia had a point. All the years I was growing up I'd considered ours a quiet, calm little town. Suddenly, for no reason I could think of, we'd had arsons, petty thefts and public disturbances, and murders right and left.

"I did some reading about serial killers," I told her. "From what I've learned, the Night Terror is right on schedule. Almost as if he's read the books and followed the profiles."

"Maybe he has," Delia said. "On-the-job training? But it seems there were some changes in his method over in Benton Harbor. If Clara can be believed."

"Clara tells everything she knows to everybody, then swears us all to secrecy," I said with a chuckle. "This was a black woman. And Clara said it was worse. I gather she means the mutilation?"

"Changed his pattern," Delia said, almost to herself. "You know, Jack the Ripper did more damage with each of his victims. I'm sure psychologists have an explanation for that. I wonder if he will disappear now and never be heard from again." She didn't have to be more specific; the terms *he* and *him*, when spoken in a certain hushed manner, always meant the Night Terror.

"He's out of Jesus Creek, at least. Maybe after Nita's funeral, we can all get back to workaday concerns, like the parade and the grand marshal and what to make for dinner."

"I certainly hope you're right. Speaking of workaday, look what's coming on your left."

I looked up to see Roger boogying toward us. Until then, I'd had no idea that he possessed an ounce of rhythm, but his arms were swinging and his body was gently rocking from side to side as he moved. What's more, he seemed to be *whistling* a rap number.

"Like a hummingbird," Delia said, "he doesn't know the words."

Roger heard her and clapped one hand to his chest. "Do you doubt me, woman? Of course I know the words." And then he began to rap in earnest. "There's a guard on duty/ and his name is Ned./ And under that sheet/ there's more than a bed."

"Stop!" I said, covering my ears. Skinny white men have no business trying to be cool.

But Roger went on. "Come St. Patrick's Day/ we'll get to see/ the hero who's known/ only to me." He ended with a little soft shoe and a flourish of arm waving.

Delia tapped my shoulder and said, "I think he's finished now. You can relax."

I uncovered my ears and looked warily at Roger. "This isn't a new hobby of yours, is it?"

"I gather you don't care for popular music."

"Who's Ned?" Delia asked.

"Actually, it's Harley Jones and Wayne Holland, but those names are hard to rhyme."

"Harley Jones?" Delia and I said together, and then Delia went on. "You think it's wise to let Harley go armed, Roger?"

Harley is a charming man. Really he is. But he has an old hunting rifle that he pulls out on occasion and uses to shoot at anything that moves on or near his property.

"He's only got a big stick today," Roger assured us. "And he seems to be a bit more . . . sane than usual."

"I have to see this," I said, rising. "Harley without his gun. And sane! What a concept!"

Roger and Delia were snuggling together on her porch as I headed back down the street toward the U that officially turns Morning Glory Way into Primrose Lane. And then, of course, Primrose heads north again. Sometimes I think it's a metaphor for life in Jesus Creek—you just keep going in circles, no matter how far you travel.

The park is cradled inside the U, so it can be claimed by both streets, not that anyone wants to claim it. It's not much of a park, anyway. Just a couple of maple saplings and now the new statue. The St. Pat's parade always begins at the courthouse and travels down Morning Glory, then back up Primrose to the courthouse again. At that point, all hell breaks loose, with parade entries shooting off in all directions. This year, of course, the parade would halt at the park long enough for the unveiling, before continuing the route.

Sure enough, Harley was out, warily circling the statue and carrying a stick that could have belonged to Buford Pusser. I doubted that any potential statue peekers would want to tangle with him. Wayne was holding down his side of the park admirably, while still keeping one eye on Harley. I was glad to see someone had warned him about the need for that.

Across the street Eliza Leach was puttering around in her yard with a hand trowel. I say puttering because there was no way she could have been doing yard work without grass or flowers. But Eliza likes to get a jump on nature. I called "Good morning" to her and she straightened to look at me. Eliza, unlike most folks around here, will not wave to just anyone. She has to check your social status first.

After ascertaining that I was, if not socially acceptable, at least not white trash, she waved half-heartedly.

"Is Sarah Elizabeth home this morning?" I asked.

Eliza took a moment to think it over, finally deciding that Sarah Elizabeth was, indeed, at home. "I'll call her out for you," she said, thus preventing me from going inside her home.

Sarah Elizabeth appeared in the doorway almost as soon as her mother-in-law called out her name. She was dressed in an elegant blue dress that flowed over her rounded belly and made her look like pregnant women are supposed to look. That is, radiant.

"Mother Eliza," she said firmly, "it's chilly outside. Here, put on this jacket. And it's almost time for church. Hadn't you better come in and get dressed?"

"Plenty of time," Eliza snapped back. But she snatched the jacket from Sarah Elizabeth's hand and went on inside, presumably to dress and apparently forgetting all about me.

Sarah Elizabeth watched her go, a tiny frown creasing her face. Almost absently she said to me, "What are you doing out so early in the morning?"

"Enjoying the weather," I told her. "I think everybody is. Delia was on her porch when I passed by, and Harley's over there prancing around." I waved one arm toward the park across the street. "Don't let me keep you if you need to help Eliza."

Sarah Elizabeth sighed. "I doubt I could help her if I tried. Have you noticed anything unusual about Mother Eliza lately, Kay?"

Well, of course I couldn't tell her that I'd always found Eliza to be a bit different, so I said tactfully, "In what way?"

Sarah Elizabeth shook her head. "I'm not sure.

Maybe it's just me, but she seems distracted and forgetful. I suppose she does have a lot on her mind, all things considered."

"That could well be," I agreed. With Sarah Elizabeth expecting Eliza's first grandchild while the father, Eliza's son, was not around to handle the paternal duties, it could be that life in the Leach household was more stressful than normal. "Maybe she's worried about you and the baby and doesn't want to let you know."

"So as not to upset me? Sometimes I think she goes out of her way to do that." There was just a trace of bitterness in Sarah Elizabeth's voice, something I'd never have expected from her. And then, apparently noticing it herself, Sarah Elizabeth allowed her face to relax, and she gave me a resigned smile. "Or maybe I'm just moody. I swear, if I'd known what a witch I'd turn into during pregnancy, I'd have boarded myself up in my room for the whole nine months."

"That would *really* make you crabby. They say it's best to keep busy. I guess it's supposed to keep your mind off how miserable you are." She certainly looked miserable, but in my opinion, all pregnant women did.

"At least I'm healthy," Sarah Elizabeth said. "My aches and pains are just the normal ones. If only people would stop telling me horror stories . . ."

"Like?"

"Oh, like the one that goes, 'I was in labor for fifteen days and they wouldn't give me a thing for the pain.' "

I was appalled. "You mean they let women go through *that*?"

"Of course they don't. Some women just like to scare the pants off the rest of us, so they come up with these ridiculous stories. That's not even the

worst one." Sarah Elizabeth seemed to be taking it
in stride, so I didn't ask her if she was sure the
accounts were false.

Instead I ordered her to go inside and prop her
feet up until time to leave for church. If there's one
thing I can't stand, it's to see a pregnant woman
standing when she could be sitting.

The Leach house was the wonder of Primrose
Lane—tall columns reaching up to the third floor,
the yard carefully landscaped. The other houses
along the street were built in another century, in a
time when elegance was defined differently. I liked
the little square numbers myself. They nestled into
the yards behind forsythia bushes and trees that
had grown up with at least two generations of children. And their owners were outside, too, but unlike Eliza, they were mostly porch sitting rather
than gardening.

After sending Sarah Elizabeth inside to tend to
her mother-in-law, I decided to chance stirring the
wrath of Roger and walked across the street to distract the guards. One of them, anyway.

"You look like a man who's been too long without sleep," I said to Wayne.

He flashed a charming grin and admitted it. "I
seem to get my best rest on dates."

I did not feel that correcting him (it was an *outing*, after all) would be in the best interest of my
future social life. "How long are you stranded here
with Harley?"

Wayne cast a wary glance over his shoulder to be
sure Harley couldn't hear us. "Till noon. If General
Lee over there doesn't shoot me first."

"I don't want to alarm you, but it could happen.
Watch him."

"Oh, believe me," Wayne said firmly, "I'm keeping an eye on that one. And as soon as possible, I'm

getting out of here and into bed. You know, it's decent of you not to fuss about me falling asleep on you yesterday."

"Hey, I've worked midnights once or twice. Don't worry about it." We stood there for a few minutes pretending to admire the tarp-covered statue. "You'd better watch out for Roger's statue, too. No telling what he's got under there."

I'd started to ease my way back to the sidewalk, but Wayne stopped me. "Hey, Kay," he called. "You like fishing?"

"Uh, yeah. I guess. I've never actually caught one, but—"

"I'm off Wednesday and Thursday. When's *your* next off day? I thought we might go down to the creek."

He was cute as a bug. You'd have thought he was a teenager asking out a girl for the first time the way he blushed.

"Thursday," I said, heading down the sidewalk. "Pick me up at ten!"

I waved and chatted with different folks on my way home, all of us seemingly obsessed with discussion of the weather, as if we were amazed that the skies had finally cleared and the air warmed. We all knew better than to count on it, though. This sort of thing happens almost every March in Jesus Creek. We get fired up about planting or picnicking or washing cars for a couple of days, and then winter returns to remind us who's boss.

Roger's house was the last on the street, just behind Proctor's Gas Station. He'd moved in less than a month before, which accounted for the absence of curtains at the windows. He was still over at Delia's, of course. Poor Roger. He could have had a wonderful time swapping weather lies with his neighbors. According to him, Chattanooga has snow deep enough to bury a house, heat enough to cook a live cow, and more rain than was originally needed to form Earth.

I took Main Street back home, thinking only briefly of stopping in at Eloise's for a doughnut. It sounded good, but I was in the mood for open air and sunshine.

John was just getting into his car when I got home. He stopped when he saw me coming, got back out of the car, and slammed the door. "It's only nine A.M.," he said with mock surprise. "And you're breathing?"

"Thought I'd try something new. Where are you off to?"

"I'm spending my morning at Scott's. We're going to plan his class schedule for the next couple of years and discuss his options."

"If you can get that boy to stay in school for two more years, you're a miracle worker."

"He's listening to me now, Kay. You ought to have more faith in people. The boy just needs a guiding hand, someone to appreciate him."

"I'm trying, John. And I'll admit I like him better than I did at first. Teenagers are awkward to talk to, you know? But he seemed vastly improved the last time he was over here. If only he wouldn't look at me like I'm to blame for all his troubles."

"He has to blame someone. Want to ride out there with me?"

"Do you think I could help convince Scott to stay in school?"

John grinned. "You just can't keep up the hard-ass facade, can you?"

Before I could reply, he said, "You could talk to Scott's mother. She'd probably enjoy that."

Never let it be said that I failed in my codependent duty. I thought Scott's mom could probably use a friendly chat. I walked around to the passenger side, prepared to think positive thoughts about the family, but my attention was caught by the uneasy position of the car.

"John," I said, "you have a flat."

As if he doubted my word, John walked around the car to look for himself. Satisfied that my assessment of the situation was correct, he pulled a ring of keys from his pocket and opened the trunk. "You don't know how to change a tire, do you?" he asked.

"Nope. The few times I've had flat tires, I just drove it over to the gas station and let Mr. Proctor handle it."

John handed me the lug wrench. "Good. Then today won't be wasted. You'll have learned something."

He had to clear out the trunk before he could pull the spare loose. John tries to be prepared for every situation, which is why his trunk contained a tool kit, a bottle of water, a pair of old sneakers, one of the ubiquitous bread wrappers, toilet paper, a hatchet, and a ratty-looking blanket. He piled all of it together on one side and pulled the loose spare out, then rolled it along the sidewalk to the front of the car.

It took twice as long as it should have taken to change the tire because John made me do it. I told him I could learn just as well by watching, but he didn't fall for it. When I discovered that the lug nuts on the flat tire had been put on by an impact wrench (a new term John taught me), I explained rationally that I didn't have the arm strength to remove them. John told me to jump up and down on the wrench. I did, but I didn't like it, especially after the neighbors came out to watch.

CHAPTER
18

The Star: You can hear the whisper of truth by listening to silence.

BY THE TIME THE CAR WAS READY TO ROLL, I needed a shower. John convinced me to settle for washing my hands and changing my jeans, which were covered with grease and tire black. Cleaned and re-dressed, but still feeling slightly annoyed with him, I crawled into the car at last, regretting that I'd agreed to go along to visit Scott and family.

As we drove out Main Street to the east, the sun rose higher in the sky as if developing more and more confidence in its ability to shine. The breeze continued, and here and there along the highway I noted slight patches of hardy grass already beginning to green.

Dead Branch Road is about a mile out of town, just short of the school parking lot. The road is gravel and narrow and winds its way through several miles of woods and farmland. There are only a few houses out that way. They're the remnants of dreams brought into the county by settlers in the eighteenth and nineteenth centuries. Most of them were homes to generations of farmers who, in the last thirty years, had been forced to sell off land parcel by parcel to stay afloat.

Along the way we passed the occasional house trailer or square-frame dwelling thrown up in the middle of a barren, treeless plot. Scott lived in one of the latter. About ten miles out, John turned into the rutted driveway and cut the engine.

The yard was mostly packed dirt. Grass would not grow there even when the year was more advanced. A rusty, mud-splattered orange Pinto sat next to the back door, between the house and a makeshift doghouse. The house had no porches, no trees in the yard, no flower boxes along the bare windows. If I hadn't been used to seeing places just like it, I'd have thought it was vacant.

John and I got out and picked our way carefully past the bicycle pieces, dog poop, stray toys, and empty flowerpots. Still no sign of life.

"Are you sure they're expecting us?" I asked, as John tapped confidently on the flimsy storm door.

"Of course," he said, apparently oblivious to appearances.

To prove him right, the door opened suddenly. Behind it stood a woman who looked as if she'd already worked a double shift and was just about ready to drop. No taller than me, she carried just enough extra weight to be plump. Even a fashion-impaired moron like myself could have told her that knit pants were uncalled for.

She smiled pleasantly, though, and pushed the storm door open. "Come on in," she said. "I was hoping you wouldn't forget. I've already got breakfast on the stove."

John introduced her as Lola and explained that

I was a friend of both his and Scott's. I thought that
was a great exaggeration, but let it go. After all, I
was beginning to tolerate Scott, and even if he
didn't yet consider me a friend, I was sure he'd come
around in time.

"Why don't you two come on into the kitchen and
we'll talk while I get the biscuits made up?" The
kitchen was visible from the front door, separated
from the living room only by a half wall. Every sur-
face in the place was covered with stacks of maga-
zines, notebooks, half-completed needlework projects,
or toys. The house was far too warm for my comfort,
and the heavy odor of cooking meat nearly strangled
me. I believe that a lived-in look makes a house a
home, but this was too much.

We followed Lola through the would-be arch of a
door and seated ourselves, at her insistence, at the
kitchen table.

I was grateful, actually, that we were sitting in
the kitchen. The living room had been decorated
with a black plastic sofa and matching chair. Both
of those pieces were partially covered with quilts,
no doubt to hide tears in the fabric. I suspected
there might be some vermin hiding in there, too,
when I spied the drooling mutt curled up in the
corner. A couple of mismatched tables and a portable television on a metal stand were the only
other substantial pieces in the room.

The walls were loaded down with framed school
photos of Scott and his two younger sisters, more of
the needlework classics that had obviously been
produced by Lola, and dozens of landscapes painted
by that ubiquitous artist whose work appears in
Wal-Mart outlets.

The kitchen blended beautifully with the decor
throughout. The table was covered first by a plastic
tablecloth, and then by an assortment of items that

probably were worth a great deal to Lola but had no place better to be. She'd shoved all that into the center of the table in order to make room for us to eat.

"Scott and the girls aren't up yet," she said, as she patted out biscuit dough on the counter. "I hollered for 'em when I heard you drive up, so they ought to be in here directly. I've got coffee made. Would you like a cup?"

John leapt to his feet and offered to pour, obviously relieved to find that he wasn't going to have to go cold turkey.

"Such a nice day," Lola said, glancing out the window. "I expect it'll get worse, though. Are you a teacher, too, Kay?"

The sudden and thoroughly unexpected question caught me off guard. "I'm a waitress," I said, feeling as if I'd disappointed her.

From the back of the house I heard the sounds of children bickering. Lola heard it, too, and screeched at them to quiet down. I assumed, from the tenor of the voices, that these were Scott's younger sisters. I'd expected them to be teenagers, too, but when they finally piled into the kitchen, I saw that they were barely school-age.

"Melissa and Angela, can you say hello to Scott's teacher?" Lola asked them.

"Hello!" they both shouted together, then collapsed into near-hysterical laughter. I, obviously, had missed the joke.

"Where's Scott?" Lola asked them, when they finally got quiet.

"In bed," one of the girls said shortly. "He said he wasn't getting up."

"Well, go tell him Mr. Sullivan is here," Lola ordered.

"He don't care," said the smaller child, "because he's sleeping and he said he wasn't getting up."

"Excuse me," Lola said to us, wiping her hands on a dish towel. "I'll go give him a shake." She disappeared down the hall, leaving us to make small talk with the two girls.

"Are both of you in school?" I asked, somewhat inanely. On the other hand, I figure children expect to be asked that question, and I didn't want to disappoint them.

"Uh-huh," the smaller girl said, and promptly stuck her thumb in her mouth.

"Angela's just in first grade," the other girl said. "I'm in third."

"Well. And do you like school?" Another question children expect to be asked.

"You know what I like best about school?" Melissa asked.

"Recess!" she and Angela shouted at the same time, once again succumbing to giggles.

By the time they'd calmed themselves, Lola had returned to the kitchen, her mouth set in a wrinkled frown. "Scott was up real late last night," she explained. "I'm having a hard time rousting him out of bed this morning."

John rose confidently from his chair. "I'll talk to him."

I almost protested, but John was gone before I had the chance. Lola, on the other hand, didn't seem to mind at all that he'd taken charge of her son. If anything, she seemed relieved.

Angela and Melissa crawled into John's chair, fighting over who would sit in whose lap. Melissa being the larger, she won and cuddled Angela like a baby doll while they both watched me the way vultures watch dying animals.

"I don't think Scott has told me where you work,

Lola," I said, casting around desperately for conversational material.

"I set collars at the shirt factory in Benton Harbor," she said, shoving a pan of biscuits into the oven. "I've been there about six years now. Since just after Angela was born."

"I thought about applying for a job there. I hear it pays well after you make production." That was true. I'd also thought about being an astronaut, a movie star, and a ditchdigger. "I don't think I'd have liked working in a factory, though. Too structured for my taste."

"Oh, it's not too bad. The floor ladies don't give you much trouble usually."

She had bacon and sausage frying in an iron skillet and was pulling plates down from the cabinet. "Girls," she said, "take these over there and set the table."

Angela and Melissa fought their way out of the chair and obeyed. I was about to offer my help when John returned, grinning triumphantly. "Scott will be here in a minute," he said. Without asking, he began to help the girls set the table.

"I'm sure glad you can do something with him," Lola said with a sigh. "You're the first teacher he's ever had a good word for."

"I think Scott and I understand each other pretty well," John told her. He'd located the cabinet that held glasses and cups and began placing those on the table. "You girls want milk, right?" he asked.

"Coke!" they shouted together.

I flinched at the thought, but since Lola didn't seem disturbed, I decided their breakfast libations were none of my business. You'd think a mother would be more concerned with nutrition, though, wouldn't you?

While John and the girls put out flatware, and

Lola flipped fried eggs in a quart of oil, Scott ambled in. He was barefoot and shirtless, wearing only a dirty pair of jeans and a silver cross on a chain worn loosely around his neck. His hair obviously had not been combed, either. At first I thought this was atrocious behavior in front of guests, then chided myself for thinking like my mother. He was simply maintaining his normal habits in spite of our intrusive presence.

"Good morning, dear," Lola said to him.

Scott ignored her and sprawled across one of the chairs, scratching his head and yawning.

"What are you drinking for breakfast, Scott?" John asked.

Scott gave him a scathing look. "Whatever."

I was already sorry I'd agreed to come. The atmosphere in the house was nearly stifling. Melissa and Angela looked to me like two little Scotts in the making. Scott himself clearly wasn't impressed by our visit, and Lola was straining to pretend that all was well and we were having a friendly little gathering. Even with my limited psychological training, I could see that this was a family in distress.

By the time I'd finished all I intended to eat, I'd noticed a subtle change in Scott's behavior. Seated in the chair next to mine, he'd gradually been leaning closer and closer to me. Once when I looked over to see if he'd fallen asleep and was about to slide right out of his chair, I caught him gazing at me with what I assumed was deep interest.

Terrific, I thought. All the men in the world, and it's this one who gets a crush on me.

I tried to gently scoot my chair away from Scott without his noticing. I didn't want him to feel that I was rejecting his somewhat nebulous attempt at friendship; neither did I want to encourage him in the least.

Infatuation did not stop Scott from wolfing down his meal. Nor did it bother John, who'd caught on to what was happening and kept giving me cute little winks and grins. Only Lola and I seemed to have trouble swallowing. She was busy playing hostess—jumping up to refill coffee and the biscuit platter, urging all of us to eat, eat, eat, and, of course, trying to keep conversation going. I was simply too uncomfortable to digest without difficulty.

When the nightmarish meal was finally over, John poured himself one last cup of coffee, insisting that Lola sit and relax. Then he complimented her on her cooking, swore he'd never be hungry again, and invited Scott to join him for an after-breakfast walk.

At first I thought Scott would refuse. He seemed undecided himself. But after thinking it over and probably deciding that he couldn't effectively woo me with his mother in the room, he rose abruptly and headed for the front door without waiting for John, and without a word to his mother.

Once they were gone, Lola and I gathered dishes and began the age-old custom of cleaning up. There are rules to cleaning up. The first one is: the guest must insist on helping. Then the hostess must refuse that help. This debate continues until the guest has successfully convinced the hostess of her burning desire to scrub pots and pans, at which point the hostess gracefully allows the guest to wash. And during this ritual, they talk.

"I'm so glad Scott's taken to Mr. Sullivan," Lola said once more. "He's a bright boy. He really is. But he just doesn't want to apply himself."

"John agrees with you," I said tactfully. "Has

Scott been—uh, giving you trouble recently, or does it go back a long way?"

Lola shook her head and placed the last dried plate on the stack beside her. "He's been rough and tumble all his life. Seems like being a teenager really set him off, though. Before that he was a regular kid. You know, he'd get into trouble now and then, but nothing serious. Now all of a sudden he's skipping school, getting into fights. I just don't know what I'm going to do with the boy."

Again, I didn't feel that she wanted to hear my suggestions, so I kept quiet.

"If he only had some kind of hobby," Lola went on.

"I noticed the doghouse when we got here," I said. "Is Scott fond of animals?"

"He used to be real attached to this one dog we had," Lola said. "But it disappeared awhile back. Old Blazer in there"—she pointed to the furry heap on the floor—"lost his spirit when Scruff took off. I've been meaning to get the kids another dog to replace Scruff, but Scott doesn't seem interested. Guess he hasn't gotten over losing his pet yet."

"I know how he feels," I said. "I've got an obnoxious cat who irritates the fire out of me, but I love having her around the house."

The dishes were done, and we had only to clean the table and countertops. I scrubbed away on those while Lola put away the last few items in the drainer.

"For a while, I thought Scott might like music," she said. "Tried to get him to join the band, but he didn't like that idea."

"I wonder why not," I said absently.

"He doesn't think band is cool, I guess. But you know, those kids in band . . . you never hear about any of them being in trouble at school. I think it must be good for them to have activities like that."

Either that, I thought, or only the kids who wouldn't have caused trouble anyway join the band.

By the time Lola and I had the kitchen finished, the girls had returned to complain that each had started a fight with the other. Lola must have spent ten minutes trying to find out who hit whom first, but the girls seemed to argue in a circle. Thankfully, John stuck his head in the front door and yelled across the kitchen for me.

"Y'all leaving already?" Lola practically wailed, and I couldn't blame her for wanting us to stay. We offered a mild distraction for her children, thus removing them from her hair for a short while.

But John was giving me his follow-my-lead look, so I complied. I thanked Lola graciously for the delicious meal, said a quick goodbye to the little girls, and told all of them to visit us anytime. (Hoping that Lola would understand this was meant as a polite formality, not a bona fide invitation.)

Once we'd backed out of the driveway and started back toward home, John's first word to me was, "Shit."

"Excuse me?"

"You've captured his heart. All Scott wanted to talk about was you. Where you work, how old you are, if you're going steady with anybody. Ah, young love."

"And when did Romeo fall for me?"

"Some men take awhile to warm up," John said. "I hope you aren't going to break his heart. Now that he's found another friend, I have high hopes for his rehabilitation."

"I wouldn't break his heart for anything in the world," I assured John. "But forget about a hot and heavy romance. And I do expect him to wear a shirt at my table."

"And that necklace with the cross! I hope he knows to take it off when he's working on motors. It's long enough to be dangerous."

"How is his motorbike?" I asked. I hadn't seen it in the yard when we'd arrived.

"The kid's a genius." John shook his head, obviously stunned by this. "Just listen to this engine."

Frankly, car engines all sound alike to me, but I listened obligingly.

"You know he keeps that motorcycle of his tucked away in a shed he built out back. Takes care of it like it's a baby. I think we're onto something. Scott obviously doesn't recognize his own talent." John's voice had wandered off, the way it does when he makes a discovery that pleases him.

I knew he was counting on Scott's mechanical ability to lead them into a cure for the boy's attitude. I understood his enthusiasm, too. Even I could see that having his skill recognized could boost Scott's self-esteem.

Regretting once more my own lack of talents, I wondered if I could learn to fix cars. But that, I chided myself, was a defeatist attitude. All my life I'd heard that everyone has a talent. In keeping with my plan to improve my life, I vowed then and there to find mine. No matter how long it took. And being a realist, I knew it might take a decade or two.

John was quiet on the ride back to town, but clearly busy analyzing the new information he'd picked up about Scott. I wondered how he'd use it. Would Scott believe in his own usefulness? And would he *want* to use his ability? For all we knew, maybe Scott dreamed of being a brain surgeon or astrophysicist, rather than a top-notch mechanic.

CHAPTER

19

The Moon: Reality is cloaked in illusion.

REB GASSLER PULLED IN BEHIND US AS
John parked by the curb. Reb was dressed in civil-
ian clothes and driving his personal pickup truck,
so it surprised me to see him. He's never dropped
in for idle chitchat before.

"Hey, y'all," he said, slamming the truck's door.
The impact knocked loose some of the dirt stuck to
his mud flaps.

"What in the world are you up to, Reb?" I asked.
"In those clothes someone might mistake you for a
real person."

"If you'll offer me a cup of coffee I'll tell you all
about it." Reb allowed me to walk ahead of him up
the concrete path, while he and John dropped back
and muttered to each other. I had the unnerving
impression that they were discussing me.

They both watched me warily as I dug around my
purse for house keys, unlocked the door, and led
them inside. Once we were all settled in the kitchen

with the coffeepot brewing, I finally lost patience and demanded, "What's going on, Reb?"

He glanced quickly at John as if the two of them were in telepathic communication, then Reb turned to me. "We've gotten a complete report on the body they found in Benton Harbor. It's not one of the Terror's victims."

I was flattered that Reb felt he could share this information with me. Apparently my interest in the case had attracted his attention. Perhaps he wanted my opinion?

"Thing is," he went on, "we're a mite concerned because we *haven't* had any Terror victims turn up. Saturday being the tenth day since his last attack and all. But right now I'm more worried about you."

"You don't have to worry about me, Reb," I assured him. "I'm staying out of dark alleys and I carry a can of Mace everywhere I go." Actually, it's a can of Lady Mystique Hair Spritz.

"I'm glad to hear you're taking precautions, Kay. But let me explain the problem. The Benton Harbor woman—the one who died Saturday? Well, it seems whoever killed her left a message. On the body, you see."

Reb was struggling to avoid graphic description, but I'd have preferred to get it straight out. "Get to the point," I said. "Please."

"Somebody carved a symbol into her chest," he said quickly, then waited a beat before going on. "It was just like the one on your front door."

John was watching me like a hawk, as if he, too, thought I might faint dead away. Actually, I was feeling alert and interested and not at all frightened. Which gives you a pretty good idea of the state of denial I was in at the time.

"Well, I'll be damned," I said. "Now that's odd."

"I've been checking around, Kay. There've been

some vague rumors about devil worship around the
county. That sort of thing pops up now and again.
But if some coven is responsible for the Benton
Harbor murder, there's a chance you could be in
real danger."

"Do devil worshipers form in covens or is that
just witches?" I asked John. I figured he'd know if
anyone did.

"You're being facetious at the wrong time, Kay."

"No, really, John. I want to get the term
straight."

"Kay, I admire your guts, but I'm serious. I think
there's a possibility that this coven or clan or whatever might have you staked out. Now can you think
of anything unusual that's happened to you lately?
Besides that artwork gettin' left on your door?" Reb
leaned forward and pulled a spiral-top pad from the
hip pocket of his Levi's.

I shrugged. "No more than you'd expect around
Jesus Creek. I haven't met any new people or offended anyone that I know of. No one's glared at
me on the street. No, I can't say that there's been
a single incident."

John left the table and poured coffee for all of us,
remembering to offer condiments to Reb. "Do you
have any idea who's included in this?" he asked.
"Where'd you hear about the satanists?"

"Somebody heard it from somebody. You know
how that goes. Like I said, we get reports of dead
animals every few years and somebody claims to
have seen a bunch of robed figures in the woods,
chanting in the moonlight. Course, we never got a
dead body before."

"Gee, I guess I should be glad that some guard-
ian angel prevented them nailing Bella to my door,
huh?" I said. The thought of it made me shiver. I

made a mental note to keep the cat inside for a while.

"Be glad they didn't nail *you* to the door," Reb pointed out. "I want you to take this seriously until we find out what's going on."

"Oh, believe me. I'm taking it seriously," I promised. The caffeine got to me then and gave me a case of the jitters like I've never had before.

John had refused to leave the house for the rest of the day. Even when I suggested that we sit out in the backyard for a while to soak up that precious sunshine, he vetoed the idea. "Pay attention to Reb. You could be in danger."

So I spent the rest of the afternoon curled up on the sofa with a legal pad and pencil, revising some old poems, while John read one of the serial-killer books I'd checked out of the library.

By five o'clock I was starving. "Look, one of us has to bring food into this house," I told John. "And I'm not allowed to walk the streets alone anymore. Why don't we order a pizza from The Drink Tank and you can pick it up."

John conceded that food was a good idea and called in the order while I put a final line to a poem that would knock some editor's socks off. "It'll be ready in twenty minutes," he told me, putting down the receiver. "I'll wait fifteen, then drive over and get it."

"Drive? You could walk, you know. A little exercise is good for mind, body, and soul."

"Yes, but driving will be faster and I don't want to leave you here alone any longer than necessary."

"John," I said, overwhelmed by his protectiveness, "you can't stick to me forever. Besides, I promise to lock all the doors behind you."

"I'm driving," he insisted.

And he did. But not before checking all the window locks himself and waiting outside to hear the tumblers when I locked the door.

I decided that while he was away, I might as well type up a couple of my new poems and get them in the mail the next day. I hate to leave a new creation sitting around.

The typewriter wasn't on John's bedside table where he usually keeps it, so I had to bend over and check under his bed. It was obviously not anywhere else in the room; all the surfaces were bare and dust-free.

Not finding it there, I checked the closet, fully expecting all John's disorganized genes to have led him into stuffing it full of items that he didn't have places for in his orderly room. I even ducked a little as I opened the door, to avoid the barrage of junk I just knew would be in there.

The closet was even tidier than the room itself. Clothes were hung together on one side of the closet, shoes were lined up snugly on the floor, and the two shelves just above the clothes bar were fully but neatly covered with labeled boxes and bags.

Only John, I thought, would stack empty bread wrappers so neatly. And then I realized they weren't empty. So he'd found a use for them after all.

For a second I considered closing the closet door and respecting his privacy, but the setup was so ludicrous, I just couldn't resist.

Taking one of the bags from the lower shelf, I weighed it in my hand. Extremely light. And yet, so carefully wrapped and stored. What on earth, I asked myself, had John started collecting now?

I gently unrolled the plastic, trying to get a glimpse of whatever was inside, but the words *Whole Wheat* printed on the bag obscured my view. I wasn't going to be able to identify anything without taking it out of the bag. So I reached in and dug around the bottom of the wrapper until I felt something thin and hard. I pulled it out.

For just a moment I thought John had gone completely mad. Why would anyone, I wondered, keep leather so carefully wrapped and stored?

And then I saw the fingernail. I almost didn't recognize it, and even when I knew—knew without any doubt—that I was holding in my hand a severed finger, I still didn't believe it. It was absurd. I considered the possibilities: a plastic finger for Halloween disguise, a potato miraculously grown to resemble a human digit. And all this time, I stood there with it in my hand, refusing to believe what was obviously the truth.

When I could deny it no longer, I did not, as you might expect, scream or throw the finger across the room. Instead, I dropped it back into the bread bag and rerolled the plastic wrapping. As casually as a housewife would place the clean towels in the linen closet, I returned the package to its shelf and gently closed the door.

Without thinking about it, I'd already decided to ignore the situation. I would not ask John what he was doing with a human finger in his closet, nor would I inspect the other packages to see what he kept in them.

I don't know what I thought would come of my denial of the facts. Obviously it was not a situation that could be ignored indefinitely. But that did not occur to me just then.

Calmly and confidently, I turned to leave the room. That's when I saw John standing in the doorway, a large white pizza box in hand. He was leaning against the door frame, smiling at me as if he'd just popped in to say hello.

"I'd never have taken you for a snoop," he said.

"Sorry. I couldn't find the typewriter." Perhaps you wonder why *I* remained so calm. The answer is simple, if stupid. It never occurred to me that there might be a problem.

Codependents can ignore anything with practice. And I'd had plenty.

"Why don't we take a drive?" John said quietly.

And only then did I feel that flush of adrenaline that tells ordinary animals they're about to become someone's dinner. My body froze; my tongue went numb. My brain, until now vacationing in Tijuana, suddenly returned to town and began screaming orders at me. Unfortunately, I was physically unable to respond to any of them. And I kept wondering what the hell he'd done with my typewriter.

"Uh, no. I don't think that's a good idea. Pizza might get cold, and boy, am I starved!" Trying to focus my thoughts just then was like dragging a horse through mud. A million ideas were rolling around in my head, and I was acutely aware that none of them had anything to do with my present dilemma. I suspected that it was yet another form of denial and regretted not having paid more attention to that workshop on facing up to unpleasantness I'd attended a few months back.

"It's a nice night," John went on, still standing there at the door. "Let's take a ride out to the river. We'll eat the pizza there."

"But I'm hungry now," I said lamely. "And I've got all this stupid paperwork to finish. I need the typewriter."

I watched John's face closely. There was absolutely no change in his expression as he stepped inside the room and placed the pizza box carefully on his bed. He gently took my hand. "All work and no play," he reminded me as he pulled me across the room.

As we entered the hallway, I noticed immediately that the linen closet door was ajar and a stack
of towels had dropped to the floor. It didn't take a
rocket scientist to make the connection—John had
removed the gun from its hiding place.

"You probably have some questions to ask me."

I stared at him, at his eyes, which were watching
me with more tenderness than any human has ever
shown me before and at the gun held casually in
his hand.

"Yes," I said, thinking that I'd finally come to
my senses. "This is serious, isn't it?" I looked at
him for confirmation, but he didn't say anything.
"You think that I think you've got a finger in your
closet. And I'll admit, it looks so much like a finger
that I can't help believing that's what it is. But I'd
like to hear your explanation."

"I'll give you an explanation while we're driving."

"But I want the truth," I said firmly, as if talking
to a child who'd offered to reveal the name of the
culprit responsible for the broken window.

"I never lie to you, Kay," John said, and continued nudging me through the hall to the living room.

I wondered briefly if he would use the gun and
decided not to chance it. Once we were in the car
and moving, he wouldn't be able to cover me and
drive at the same time. I was certain I could leap
from a moving vehicle and run for help, if need be.
But I still wasn't convinced that John would hurt
me.

"You found a finger?" he began. He took my
purse from the front closet and handed it to me as
we stepped onto the porch.

I nodded.

"How many packages are there in my closet?"

I tried to remember how the stacks had looked,

so that I could form a close estimate. "I don't know. Quite a few, I'd say."

"Twenty," he said, almost proudly. "Each one contains a piece, a souvenir. You understand what I'm talking about, of course."

"Not exactly," I admitted. And with a nervous giggle I added, "At the moment, the only explanation seems to be that you've been killing people and collecting their body parts."

"Well, you told me to get a hobby."

That line cinched it for me. Surely, I explained to myself, if John had real body pieces in his room, he wouldn't be making jokes about it. I smiled back at him, greatly relieved. "Yes, I did suggest it. So what is it that you're collecting, John?"

"Memories," he said plainly. "Just like some people collect towels from hotels to help them remember a good vacation, or others take pictures. My little moments of joy are in those bags. I can tell you everything about each one—what she wore, what we talked about. Sometimes I like to just hold them in my hands and relive the conversations."

So calm was he that I began to suspect I'd imagined it all. Had I gone so far around the bend that I was seeing things that weren't there? I decided to tread lightly, hoping that he would give me a cue before I made a colossal ass of myself. I now refer to this as my blackest moment of codependence— ignoring what I'd seen and *knew* to be true, I was prepared to believe any lie John could conjure.

He held my arm at the elbow and steered me down the front walk to the car. Carefully glancing around, I found all the neighbors' yards empty. No help there. I considered breaking away from him and running down the street. I thought perhaps I could scream like a banshee and frighten John into retreat until someone arrived to rescue me.

But he seemed to read my mind. He tightened his grip and shoved me into the car on the passenger side. Then he slid in beside me, forcing me to move behind the wheel.

"You want me to drive? John, you hate the way I drive." I was frantic now. But maybe I could still jump out, during a slow curve or—

"And be sure to wear your seat belt." John pointed to it with the gun.

There was little choice. Seat belt fastened, engine running, I eased the car away from the curb and prayed for another plan.

"You want to know about my trophies?" he said at last.

I nodded. Trophies. The word was so bizarre that it didn't register with me for a second, and when it did I knew that I'd made a horrible mistake. Those were not body parts at all. Silly me. I'd mistaken little statues for—

"You see, I like to remember," John was saying. "The way you keep that scrapbook on your dresser."

I tried to make the connection between his mementos and mine. "I think," I said, slowly and with growing certainty, "that you're a sick man. Tell me in complete sentences just exactly what those things in the closet are. And where did they come from?" I was growing more and more certain John was not the man I'd thought, but I desperately needed to hear it from him. Or hear a denial.

"I think we should talk this through, John. You do understand that you're in serious trouble, don't you?" I was running on the assumption, now, that things were as bad as I could possibly imagine. Otherwise, why wouldn't John simply give me an answer to clear it all away?

"I wallow in trouble like a hog wallows in mud." He grinned devilishly.

"John. You've got to take responsibility for this. I can't think straight. Who should we contact? The police, certainly, but maybe first we should call a counselor or a minister. You know, someone who can explain to the police that you've got a problem, that you aren't responsible for what you've done."

John leaned over and planted a delicate kiss on the top of my head. "How convenient of you to cover for me. But of course I'm responsible."

"You don't know what you're saying, John. No sane person would kill a string of women and keep relics around for just anyone to find."

Now right about here every reality-denying cell in my body got up and left. In clear, stark, sharp-edged stereo, my brain picked up on what was happening. Yes, finally. And perhaps I was dumb to have taken so long. But answer truthfully: if someone told you your roommate was a serial killer, would *you* believe it?

CHAPTER
20

The Sun, reversed: The highway is shrouded by fog; the Fool should tread carefully.

JOHN HELD THE GUN IN HIS RIGHT HAND, and would occasionally use his left to pat my arm reassuringly. I didn't dare take my eyes off the road to look over at him. Driving was difficult enough, what with my shaking legs and night blindness.

I was terrified that John wanted to take me out to some deserted glade and show me a dead body. He'd been completely silent as I drove up Morning Glory toward the other side of town and the creek for which our town is named.

"Where are we going?" I asked at last, desperate to end the eerie quiet.

"Riding," John said enigmatically.

"If you're really the Night Terror," I challenged him, "then why didn't you kill someone yesterday? Or has the body not been found yet?"

"I was bored with the predictability of it. And besides, the police were getting far too complacent.

It seemed like a good time to stir them up a little. Turn left up here." He indicated the cross street between Morning Glory and Primrose, just north of the town. "Straight across to the old river road."

If Wayne had chosen a neglected byway to get us to Plant the day before, John was about to go him one better. The old river road hasn't been used for traffic in half a century. It's kept graded and graveled only as far as the Tyler house driveway, but since no one's lived there in years even the first few yards were rough going.

When we passed the Tyler house, it was dark. The new owners must have been out for the evening, or perhaps they'd made the wiser decision to get out of town before the Jesus Creek curse struck them, too.

"I don't think we can go too far on this road," I pointed out truthfully. "It's nothing but ruts and holes from here on."

"Keep going," John said.

I'd had to slow to barely five miles per hour to prevent serious damage to the car, and still we were bouncing around like Mexican beans. Once or twice I heard John's head hit the top of the car.

Suddenly he said, "It's odd to be in the passenger seat. I've been the driver for so long, cruising the highways and carrying women to their destinies. It's fitting that we do it differently this time." He reached out and took my right hand off the steering wheel. I was sure he could tell from my sweaty palm how nervous I was. "I wanted you to be special, Kay. You know, I wouldn't have hurt you for the world."

I wasn't happy with the way he used the past tense there.

"Well, John, I certainly wouldn't hurt you either. Which is why I think it's important that we get you some help. We'll find out why you feel compelled to do these terrible things. I'm sure it will be fine."

John released my hand and placed it gently back on the wheel. "You want me to explain how I was traumatized as a child? We could lay the blame on my mother. God knows I'd get sympathy with that story!"

"Yes," I said tenderly. "I know you've suffered. And other people will understand, too. You've been trying to work through that, but you've expressed your anger inappropriately, John."

He laughed as if I'd told the best joke in the world. "Inappropriate expression of anger. I might use that if they ever catch me."

"*If* they—" I was stuck. Surely he planned to turn himself in. Or maybe I hadn't made myself clear. "There are people who can help. Just like you've helped Scott. And I'm always here for you, John."

"You'd be willing to fix me, is that it? But, Kay, I don't consider myself broken. You think I've got a warped morality, that it can be turned around and made to look just like yours. The truth is, I've got a clear picture of what this universe is all about. I don't believe in the wrath of God. I don't believe that suffering makes me strong. But I'm absolutely certain that the best we can do in life is to make ourselves happy."

I'd spent enough time in therapy groups, and read all the informative brochures. Up to a point, I'd thought I could talk to John on his slightly skewed level and make him see that there were steps to be taken. Now I'd lost the thread of his logic completely.

"You can't believe that it's all right to kill people. Why would you want to do something like that?"

"Because I like it," he said simply. "It's power.

It feels good. And there's such pure joy in the clean getaway. Which, as you may have noticed, I've mastered."

"No, you haven't mastered it. As much as I care for you, I can't ignore this. As soon as we get back to town I'm calling Reb. I really believe that it will be easier for you if you tell him this story yourself."

Out of the corner of my eye I could see John shake his head. "You won't be going back to town, Kay."

Oh. I processed this statement with a calmness that was so unnatural I began to wonder if John's insanity had infected me. But I also recognized that my clear head was an asset at the moment. "You're planning to kill me," I said, just a bit sarcastically. "Frankly, I think you'd need my help to do it. How are you going to explain my sudden disappearance?"

John thought a minute. "I've got several choices. I could say you insisted on going for a walk after dinner and never came home. Your body won't be found for a while, and when it is, the Night Terror won't be the first suspect. You realize, of course, that this satanist angle is a perfect setup."

"*You* put that pentagram on the door?"

"No, no, no," he said. "I had nothing to do with the pentagram. Apparently you've really been targeted by the local demon squad."

"Then why do you want to kill me?" I was frightened, yes. But more than that, I was hurt by his betrayal of our friendship.

"I don't want to. Didn't I just tell you how very much I care about you, Kay?"

We hit another major rut, and I felt my brain rattle around in my head. "You've confused me. I thought you said you were planning to kill me."

"Yes, but I don't *want* to do it. I just don't have

a choice. If I'd kill for fun, I'd kill to protect my-self." He chuckled. "Pull over here."

I did as he said and pulled to the side of the road, leaving the car running.

"Cut the engine," he instructed, and I obeyed. "We have to go around to the trunk."

My legs were trembling and all the blood drained from my head as I stood up. For a second I think I actually lost consciousness, but before I could faint, John had taken my arm and was leading me around to the back of the car. Keeping the gun aimed at my head, he let go of my arm to open the trunk. Then he reached in to grab the blanket that was rolled up in one corner. Shaking it gently, he re-leased the items that had been hidden in it—an empty bread wrapper and my long-lost Ginsu knife.

"Amazing invention," he said, holding the knife up for me to see. "I never have to sharpen it."

Utter terror had turned my mind into a top-notch machine. I was computing options faster than warp speed and rejecting them just as quickly. The Tyler house was the only residence within two miles, and even it was empty. The road was flanked on both sides by overgrown woodlands and probably stag-nant pools from the creek overflow. John had the car keys in his pocket. I was in his clutches, liter-ally, and I didn't think there was a chance in hell of finding a white knight in the vicinity.

"There's something I've always wanted to know," John said. "What goes through a victim's mind just before she dies? What are you thinking right now, Kay?"

"Honestly?" I said. "I'm thinking that I'm in deep trouble."

"Where's your sense of poetry? Aren't you con-sidering the possibility of life after death at the very least?"

"Look, John, you want poetry, you send me roses.
I have known you and shared with you and, by God,
even loved you. And what I feel right now is fury. Now
either kill me and get it over with or die and go to
hell, but don't expect me to play silly games."

The moon had disappeared behind a cloud, and
the darkness on that road was so thick I could
barely see him. But I thought there was a sadness
in his eyes, and it gave me an instant of hope.
Maybe he'd been fooling himself. Surely he cared
as much about me as I'd once cared for him.

John brought the knife down to my throat and
laid it tenderly against my skin. "Goodbye, Kay,"
he said softly.

I realized two things in that split second: that I
was about to die, and that I was horrified by the
thought of dying alone and unnoticed. Without any
plan of action, I jerked my head to one side. This
served only to distract the aim of the blade, so that,
instead of having my jugular severed, I received a
deep and stinging cut across my shoulder. In less
than an instant, I swung with my good arm and
knocked the gun from his other hand.

John was taken off guard, though, and in the brief
moment he wasted wondering how he'd missed, I
took off. Running like the devil was after me (and
I suppose that's exactly what was happening), I
headed into the trees, hoping some batlike instinct
would lead me.

If the night was eerily silent, I didn't notice. The
sound of my own crashing and bumbling about was
driving me mad; I knew that John could follow me
by the noise I was making. But I didn't dare slow
down, not even when I ran headlong into a large
oak that jutted out of the dark in front of me. I was
concentrating on my feet, since I couldn't see anything anyway. A lifetime of television addiction had

taught me that the intended victim always sprains
her ankle during the chase, and I wasn't about to
fall into that trap.

I could hear John close behind me. The trees and
hanging vines didn't slow him down at all. In my
pitiful physical condition I should have been winded
after thirty seconds, but adrenaline was pumping
through me like wildfire.

The ground was getting soggy, and I knew I must
be running toward the creek. I had a half-formed
idea about jumping in and swimming. Unfortunately I wasn't sure just how far the creek was from
the road, nor how far I'd run. For that matter, I
could have been running in circles. It wouldn't have
surprised me to find myself back on the edge of the
road.

"Kay," John called, and I was gratified to hear
that he was a bit breathless from running. "Kay,
hold up."

He sounded pitiful, but the blood trickling down
my shirtfront reminded me that this was not the
man I'd grown to trust. I heard him swear as he
crashed into a clump of brush I'd narrowly avoided
just a second before. I said a quick prayer, asking
that John's ankle be broken.

Maybe I should have prayed a little harder. In no
time I heard his feet pounding the ground behind
me, but at least I'd gained a few feet. Unfortunately, the adrenaline rush was waning, and I
seemed to be losing blood at a much faster rate than
I'd have thought normal. Between these things and
justified panic, I was losing strength. I felt a tingle
in my spine that ran up through the back of my
neck and seemed to eat away at my brain. Reason-
ing power had deserted me. I was obsessed with the
rhythm of my own feet hitting the ground, almost
hypnotized by the pattern.

The luck that had allowed me to escape nature's little booby traps gave out, and before I realized it was there, I was pitched forward across a ditch. I landed flat on my back, the breath knocked out of me as if I'd been punched in the stomach. There was no way I was going to get to my feet and get out of there before John caught up, and I knew it. Sometimes we just have to make the best of reality.

Slowly I raised myself up on one elbow and fought for breath. The man could have followed the sound of my wheezing through a windstorm.

He was angry when he got there. Stopping at my feet, John knelt down beside me. A sliver of light from some brazen star slipped through the trees and glinted off the knife in his hand.

"You're a lot of trouble," he said accusingly. "None of the others acted this way."

"What do you expect me to do? Apologize?" I should have taken a moment to be proud of my bravado, but I was busy gasping for breath.

"I can't have you walking through the woods," he mumbled, as if thinking aloud. "You might take off again." And then, almost cheerfully, he concluded, "Oh, well. I suppose this is as good a place as any."

Supporting myself with my right arm, I was frantically clawing the ground with my other hand. I found nothing so useful as a large rock, but a good-size tree limb was just under me. I grabbed and pulled, swinging wildly as John's arm raised to strike. It was an old, dried branch, and it broke from the force of being swung. Also, I am not left-handed and my aim was completely off. But the threat of it caused John to jump back instinctively, and he lost his footing. He landed on his backside, caught himself immediately, and shifted onto his knees.

I knew that would give him more stability, and even if I'd been able to find another weapon quickly enough, it would take a tremendous blow to knock him to the ground. I kept swinging at him with the piece of branch still in my hand. Each time it made contact another piece of bark fell loose, and it quickly disintegrated.

He was fighting, too, of course, but was only able to make minimal contact. Still I could feel the burning slashes each time, and every swipe of the knife drained me a little. I knew that if I didn't get to my feet and either disable him (which seemed highly unlikely) or get the hell out of there, I would be dead in another minute.

At one point I actually considered giving in and dying. It seemed inevitable and so much easier than going on. But anger, more than fear, prevented it. I channeled all the energy left into a single fierce blow, delivered more with my fist than with what was left of my tree limb. It caught John on one side of the head and knocked his torso to one side, although he was still firmly set on his knees.

I, on the other hand, was precariously balanced by one arm, still sprawled on the ground like an old dog. I pushed with my right arm and rolled to my left, then took to my feet running. My eyes had grown accustomed to the blackness, and I was able to pick my way through the brush and around the trees better than I had before.

I mentally surveyed my body, identifying knife wounds across my chest, arms, and one that had surely laid my cheek open. It occurred to me that John had never closed the car trunk. If I could somehow figure out where the road was and run in that direction, I could at least grab the tire iron and defend myself. But I didn't have the luxury of stopping to look around. John was on my heels, tearing through the woods with the endurance of a long-distance runner.

I kept dodging trees, watching ahead of me but trying to change direction for a better look at where I might be headed. Finally I spotted a lightened area. I knew it couldn't be a house, but I thought perhaps moonlight had found its way through the clouds and was reflected off the metal of John's car. Whatever I saw, it was my only hope for salvation. I headed toward it, picking up speed with the thought that I might survive the night after all.

CHAPTER
21

Judgment: Now is the time for action.

I THINK I DISCOVERED THAT NIGHT WHAT
health nuts mean when they say they've found a
runner's high. That light through the trees was my
inspiration. I refused to consider the possibility that
it might be nothing more than moonlight on the
creek.

Instead I ran toward it, glided toward it, even
soared. I had a stride that would have made Wilma
Rudolph weep. I was dodging trees and leaping
across brush piles with the grace of Baryshnikov.
At one point I remembered a line that I'd once
heard and found ridiculous: "This is a good day to
die."

I understood it then. The wind was brushing past
my ear, drowning out the sound of everything except John's pursuit and my own pumping heart. I
was aware of the musky scent of creek mist and
night fog mingled with the odor of decaying trees.
I felt alive, tingling with the smooth movement of

my own body. It was a good night to die, but damned if I'd do it.

Bursting through the last barrier line of pin oaks and scrub, I all but fell into a small campfire on the ground. Thank God! It wasn't my imagination, nor was it a trick of moonlight. Someone was nearby, someone who would save me from the Night Terror.

Glancing frantically around for another human, I found none. Only John as he burst into the clearing after me. We both seemed surprised to see each other, as if we'd been running for the fun of it all along and hadn't expected to find another aficionado of the sport.

Then I noticed movement all around me. Dark shapes, swaying somewhat, but not in the way that trees move in the breeze. I risked a sideways glance, taking my eyes off John for only a second. To my right I spotted a half-dozen robed figures, their faces covered by dark hoods. I couldn't see their expressions, of course, only their eyes glinting through the holes cut in the hoods. But I suspected that they were stunned to silence by the sudden appearance of a blood-drenched woman and her deranged, knife-welding pursuer.

"He's the Night Terror!" I shouted, pointing to John.

The figures turned to look at him.

"Sorry, Kay. You were better off in the woods with me." A smile spread across his face. "These are the folks who left that pretty design on your door."

And this, I thought ruefully, would be what is known as hitting the wall.

Or hitting bottom. I had nowhere to go, no one to turn to. It seemed the only thing I could do was give in. "Okay," I said, with admirable calm, "fight for me then. Serial killers, satanists—nobody gets to kill me until you've agreed on a method. In the meantime, I'll just sit down here by the fire and rest."

I sunk to the ground, shaking from exhaustion and chilled from fear and loss of blood. As far as I was concerned, the evening was over. I'd put up a great fight, but even I know when to quit.

"Lady, are you serious?" One of the robed figures stepped forward. "Is this guy really the Night Terror?"

"Well, he's sure not Julia Child chasing an entrée," I snapped. "You think I'm out for a bedtime stroll? Do I look like Geraldo Rivera tracking down a lead?"

Two of the robed figures began to move cautiously toward me. I had a sinking feeling that John was not going to fight them for the right to kill me himself.

While those two knelt beside me and surveyed my numerous wounds, the other five or six (I forgot to count) inched their way toward John, warily eyeing his knife. I heard them discussing matters with each other as I drifted into a haze of apathy.

"It might be him," one of them said.

"Naw, it's not him," another responded. That one sounded familiar to me, but I was in no condition to search for a name to suit the voice.

"Doesn't matter if he's the Night Terror or not," the first said. "He's sure as hell been trying to kill this little lady. I think we'd better do something with him. Tie him up or something. We don't need this kind of trouble."

John lifted both hands in an exaggerated shrug and carefully dropped his knife to the ground. "Go for it, boys," he said.

* * *

They'd tied John's hands securely behind his back with his belt and piloted him with shoves and curses out to the road, while I was borne on the shoulders of one of the sturdier satanists. Except for an occasional whispered exchange, no one spoke a word to us as we marched along the road and up the hill to the Tyler house.

Once we were there, John was dumped on the doorstep. Most of the satanists scattered, while the one who had carried me stayed behind to pound on the door. The woman who answered the summons was clearly stunned by what she saw. One hand went to her mouth to cover a frightened gasp, the other to the silver cross hanging around her neck. But she quickly recovered herself and asked, "What's going on here?"

"Call the police, ma'am," the satanist beside me instructed. He joined his fellows, and then they all melted into the dark yard and were gone.

I smiled weakly at the poor old lady and began to explain. "This man is the Night Terror. And he tried to kill me. But that ... gentleman and his friends rescued me. And now I'd like you to call the police."

She stared at me, obviously thinking that the call should be to the loony bin instead. From the back of the house I heard a door slam and a man's voice shout, "Martha? Somebody there?"

"Dave, come in here," the woman answered.

Dave, who surely must have been her husband, was as surprised as she when he saw us lingering on his steps. I repeated my story to him, in slightly more detail, and with the graciousness of any Southern family, they helped me into the house and settled me in a chair by the fire.

They made John lie facedown on the floor, and Dave covered him with a hunting rifle just to be certain there'd be no trouble.

"Now let me get you a cup of tea," Martha said solicitously. "You poor child, you must be miserable. You're bleedin' all over the place and those clothes are filthy." She kept talking until she was out of the room, but I felt the hum of her voice as I leaned back in the chair and closed my eyes.

If I'd had energy to spare, I'd have laughed. Imagine being saved by the satanists, I thought. I supposed that John had given up only because he realized the lot of them could identify him.

"I'm sorry, Kay," John said from his prone position. "Truly I am. I barely remember any of this night. I know I tried to hurt you. I must have gone a little crazy. You know I'd never do anything like that to you." His eyes were glazed and wounded. "I'm so sorry, Kay. Really."

I felt warm from the glow of the fire, and the night had gotten a bit fuzzy for me, too. "I know, John," I said soothingly. "I understand. Don't worry. We'll get someone to help you."

And then, for an instant, John grinned at me. "Remorse, darling. It's vital. If Bundy had tried it, they wouldn't have fried him."

Before I digested his words, that baffled look was back on his face and his whole body sagged and shook with what any jury would have believed were heartfelt sobs.

CHAPTER
22

The World: The journey is ended. Now begins another journey.

JESUS CREEK TOOK ON A NEW RADIANCE after the Night Terror was captured. Oh, we were still a bit wary of walking alone after dark (some of us more than others), but all in all, I'd say the town got back to its version of normal after that.

I spent a few days in the medical center while my wounds healed. My right cheek still bears a glaring red welt from John's attack and always will. Some scars never heal.

I've received two letters from John, both of them apologetic. So far I haven't replied.

The Lady Mystique regional manager visited me in the hospital, bringing with her a Lady Mystique travel kit and a perky bouquet. She suggested that Lady Mystique Cover All would hide the scar, but I've given up wearing—and selling—makeup.

During my brief convalescence I also decided to give up my job at Eloise's and sell my house. I've applied for enrollment in the police academy. It seems I've found my calling. And if not—if this is just another side trip on the journey of life—so what?

I'm going to twelve-step meetings regularly now, and paying attention. I've decided that the trouble with me is, I think I can analyze the program and make it work. Maybe there are times when you just have to believe and see what follows.

Wayne Holland visited me in the hospital, too. Every day. He's the one who drove me home and put new locks on my doors and cooked me Hamburger Helper for dinner four nights in a row.

And the best news of all? Three of my poems will be featured in a forthcoming *Soggy Bottom Review*.

On March 17, Wayne and I were decked out in green hats and shamrock arm bands. We stationed ourselves in Sarah Elizabeth's front yard to watch the parade and witness the unveiling of Roger's statue.

Kate Yancy and her employer, the psychic, were there with us, along with Sarah Elizabeth and her mother-in-law. We stood together at the edge of the street, enjoying the clowns as they passed and the local high school band's rendition of "King of the Road."

"This town gets weirder by the minute," opined Owen Komelecki, the psychic.

"Owen's just nervous around here," Kate explained. "He almost got killed on his first visit."

"That'll make you nervous, for sure," I said. Owen Komelecki and I exchanged a look that passes only between initiates of a certain club.

"We might as well move over to the park," Owen said, before the others had time to remember that near-death experiences weren't fit conversation in that group.

"I don't think we have to do that," Kate complained. "We've got a nice shade here, and we should be able to see just fine."

"Let's go on to the park," Owen urged her. "The crowd's building up."

Reluctantly Kate and the rest of us picked our way through the band, which by this time had stopped in place for the momentous occasion at hand—the unveiling. Behind the band, the Shriners were marking out figure eights on their noisy motorcycles and Eliza was glaring at them.

I don't know if she actually hexed the riders, but just as we cleared the band, one of the motorcyclists lost control of his bike and careened into Eliza's yard, coming to a stop in the very spot where we'd been standing moments before.

Kate looked up at Owen and mouthed, "You knew."

Personally, I think it was just a coincidence.

The motorcyclist wasn't badly hurt, beyond damage to his pride, and his buddies quickly got him back on two wheels. Happily they cut their engines for the big moment.

Roger Shelton stood next to the statue, his face alight with the joy of expectation. On either side of him stood little old ladies, members of the Historical Society who'd volunteered to pull the ropes that would bring down the tarp and give us all our first glance at the hero underneath.

Delia had been offered this honor but wisely refused.

With the crowd attentively listening, Roger began his speech by pulling a wad of note cards from his pocket. I'd suspected as much. I tuned him out and waited for the veil to drop.

I caught a glimpse of young Scott through the crowd. This was the first I'd seen of him since before John's arrest. I had to wonder how Scott would be affected by the loss of his only hero.

Scott saw me and began inching his way through the crowd. At first I thought he was going to join us, but he only passed by, pausing long enough to nudge me off balance. I thought I heard him mutter, but I didn't catch the word.

I almost went after him. That old urge to comfort and heal came over me, but good sense prevailed. Some things you just can't fix.

Roger droned on and on, until Delia stepped up beside him and said, loud enough for all to hear, "Get *on* with it!"

With a dramatic hand gesture, Roger shouted out to the crowd, "I present to you today the hero of Jesus Creek."

The old ladies pulled on their ropes. The tarp came down. The crowd fell silent.

Before us stood a bullet-shaped slab of granite, smooth and formless, pointing up toward the azure sky. *I* noticed right away that it didn't look like any hero I'd ever seen. From the expressions on the faces around me, it seemed I wasn't alone in my confusion.

"No one candidate received a majority of votes," Roger explained. "The sheer number and variety of nominees convinced me that this statue must somehow attempt to honor all the heroes, both those we've recognized and those who have gone unappreciated until now."

The crowd was unimpressed by abstract art and getting restless, so with a maniacal flurry of arm waving, Roger finished. "Real heroes are hidden behind layers of the ordinary," he proclaimed. "Celebrate them wherever and whoever they are."

About the Author

Deborah Adams is an award-winning poet and short-story writer. Actively involved with Sisters in Crime, the Appalachian Writers' Association, and other writers' organizations, Ms. Adams lives in Waverly, Tennessee. Her other novels include *All the Great Pretenders* and *All the Crazy Winters*.

EDGAR AWARD WINNER

[[[SHARYN McCRUMB]]]

GIVES YOU

The Best

In Mystery